The Great
Baseball Card Hunt

The Great Baseball Card Hunt

T4874

A Southside Sluggers Baseball Mystery

Created by Glenn Lewis and Gail Tuchman
Written by Daniel A. Greenberg
Illustrated by Bert Dodson

LITTLE SIMON
Published by Simon & Schuster
New York ◆ London ◆ Toronto ◆ Sydney ◆ Tokyo ◆ Singapore

LITTLE SIMON
Simon & Schuster Building, Rockefeller Center, 1230 Avenue of the
Americas, New York, New York 10020 Text copyright © 1992 by
Glenn Lewis and Gail Tuchman. Illustrations copyright © 1992 by
Bert Dodson. All rights reserved including the right of reproduction in
whole or in part in any form.
LITTLE SIMON and colophon are trademarks of Simon & Schuster.
Designed by Lucille Chomowicz.
The text of this book is set in Stempel Garamond.
The illustrations were done in black ink.
Also available in a SIMON & SCHUSTER BOOKS FOR YOUNG READERS hardcover
edition. Series conceived and text produced by Book Smart Inc.
Manufactured in the United States of America.
10 9 8 7 6 5 4 3 2 1   (pbk) 10 9 8 7 6 5 4 3 2 1
ISBN: 0-671-72927-6   ISBN: 0-671-72931-4 (pbk)

Contents

1 The Ball Hog

The batter cracked a high fly ball to right center field. As Rachel Langlin circled beneath it, she saw someone out of the corner of her eye.

It was the left fielder—and he was coming in fast, completely out of control. "Clear out, everyone!" he yelled.

Andy West, the reserve catcher and Rachel's best friend, covered his eyes.

Zach Langlin, Rachel's younger brother, looked up at the sky from the pitcher's mound. "They're done for!" he said.

There was a gasp. Birds scattered. Just before impact Rachel thought to herself, *This is dumb.*

It was dumb. Arms and legs tangled. Rachel saw little pink stars. Bright skyrockets flashed in front of her eyes like fireworks on the Fourth of July.

As the two players untangled, Rachel moaned, "I'm hurt!" But she wasn't really. Mostly she was just dazed and angry.

The kid had actually caught the ball! He was the same athletic-looking kid who had tripled the last time he was up. And knocked one completely over the fence the time before that.

"Hi," the kid said. "I'm Seth Bradigan. The new left fielder."

Seth smoothed down his straight brown hair. Then he got up and flipped the ball to the second baseman—leaving Rachel on the ground.

"Nice grab," Rachel said out loud. Then under her breath she muttered, "Ball hog."

After practice, at the team meeting, the new coach of the Southside Sluggers had only one word to say:

"Communicate."

Rachel wrote the word "Communicate" in her baseball notebook.

"I think the Sluggers can be a good team this year," Coach Terwilliger said.

"Fat chance," Rachel wrote in her notebook.

She looked around at her teammates. Weren't these the same Southside Sluggers that won exactly two games last year and lost eighteen?

"Last year was last year," the coach continued. "Most of you were new to the league. You were learning how to play. This year you have to learn to be a team. You have to learn to communicate."

Suddenly Rachel realized what the coach was getting at.

"That collision out there in right field . . ." the coach said, shaking his head.

All eyes flashed to Seth Bradigan. Then to Rachel. Then back to Seth.

"Hey," Seth said. "Don't blame me for being a great outfielder. I *called* for that ball—loud and clear. I just made a super catch!"

"The point is, Seth," the coach said, "it was the right fielder's ball, not yours."

"Maybe," Seth said.

"*Maybe?*" Rachel cried. "You plowed right into me. You ran me over out there!"

"Look," Seth said. "The point is—I caught it. Like the great outfielder Darryl Strawberry, I get the job done. And that's all that counts!"

Rachel's eyebrows raised for a second. Darryl Strawberry was Rachel's A-Number-One all-time favorite baseball player.

"You're a good player, Seth," Coach Terwilliger said. "But remember there are other players out there too."

"Yeah," Zach Langlin piped in. "You haven't even been a Slugger for three hours and you've already run over my sister. I hope you realize she's the only one I've got!"

Seth glared at Zach.

Zach broke into a broad grin. As usual, he was trying to lighten things up. And for the moment it seemed to work.

"Look, you guys," said Coach Terwilliger. "Overall we were pretty good today. Let that carry on into the season, okay? See you Saturday at one o'clock sharp for our opening game. Got it?"

"Got it!" everyone answered.

And with that they all left in separate groups. Shortstop Ernie Peters, center fielder Susan Stein, and first baseman Marty Franklin together. Third baseman Michelle Brooks, relief pitcher Robin Hayes, and second baseman Luis Diaz together. Andy, Zach, and Rachel. And Seth all by himself.

"Obstreperous," Rachel said as they walked along Morgan Street. "Definitely obstreperous."

Andy looked at his friend Rachel. A sprinkling of red freckles dotted both cheeks and the tip of her nose. Her freckles matched her braided red hair.

Rachel's mouth had a habit of running off a bit at times like this. Leave it to Rachel to sum everything up with some word no one ever heard of before.

"What's obstreperous?" Andy asked.

"Not what—*who*," Rachel replied. "Seth Bradigan is obstreperous."

"And here I thought he was our left fielder," Zach joked.

"I still don't know what *obstreperous* means," Andy said, looking at Rachel. "*Obstreperous* must be today's word!"

"It means loud and noisy," Rachel said. "It means hard to handle. It means Seth Bradigan."

As her best friend, Andy had heard quite a few of Rachel's *words* come and go. He used to think it was weird that a fifth-grade girl would collect words the way other kids collected stamps or butterflies or baseball cards. Now he just took it for granted.

"The thing I don't get," Rachel continued, "is how a guy like Seth Bradigan could be such a fan of Darryl Strawberry's. I mean, not everyone fully appreciates Darryl Strawberry."

"I like Darryl Strawberry," Zach said.

"You're my brother. There would be no living with me if you didn't like him!"

"Well, still, Sis . . ."

"I think Darryl Strawberry is sometimes a little obstreperous himself," Andy said.

"Bite your tongue," Rachel said. "Darryl Strawberry is *not* obstreperous. Just a bit misunderstood by some people."

"Exactly my point," Andy said. "Seth Bradigan is misunderstood. Just like Darryl Strawberry."

Andy wasn't surprised to hear Rachel defend Darryl Strawberry. He was her idol. She had his poster. She had a baseball that he'd autographed. She even had a pair of D.S. batting gloves—which was remarkable because Rachel never used batting gloves.

"Anyway," Andy said in his easygoing way, "I'll bet you Seth is really an okay guy. Remember he's new here. He was probably just trying to impress us."

Andy was the peacemaker in the group. It was just like him to stick up for the new kid. He tried to look for the best in everybody.

"Hey, there must be something more important to talk about than Seth," interrupted Zach.

"Like what, little brother?" Rachel said.

"Like our team's got its season opener on Saturday," Zach said. "Aren't you guys a little worried?"

"Why worry?" Rachel said. "We lost eighteen games last year. How can we do any worse than that?"

"We could lose nineteen," Zach said with a faint smile.

"No way!" Andy said, tugging his cap down over his curly dark hair. "We're better than last year. We have a new coach who really knows baseball; you're pitching better, Zach; Robin is more effective in relief; and we're a year older. And 'the ball hog' does look like a great player."

"You make it sound like we have a shot at the championship or something," Rachel said.

"We could," Andy answered. "If we work on teamwork like Coach Terwilliger said. We have to *look* better out there."

"We do look better," Zach said. "Don't you like the new uniforms?"

Zach and Rachel's father, the team sponsor and owner of the Southside Ice Cream Shop, had recently bought new team uniforms.

"To tell the truth," Andy said, "I think they're pretty ugly."

"What's wrong with slime green on a field of sick orange?" kidded Zack. "So what if they look like joke pajamas? Dad arranged it so they match his new ice-cream flavors—Pickleberry Sundae and Orang-u-tang Chip."

"Yuck!" said Andy.

"That's the point," Zach said. "Don't you know anything about baseball? Ugly uniforms mean good teams. The uglier the uniform, the better the team."

"Not always," replied Rachel. "We have ugly uniforms and we're still the worst team in the league."

"Well we *did* win a couple of close games against the Mudsharks at the end of last season," Andy said. "And that made the Mudsharks the worst team."

"But that was only because most of the Mudsharks had chicken pox," Zach said.

"The flu," Andy corrected.

"See," Zach said. "We're so messed up we can't even keep our diseases straight."

"I can't believe this," Andy said. "Is this a team, or what? We sure could use a little team spirit."

With that Zach stuck his arms straight out.

"I . . . am the Little Team Spirit . . . of the Southside Sluggers," he announced in a ghostly wail, his eyelids fluttering spookily.

"I see the past," the Spirit said, waving its arms in the air. "It is a very sad, losing past. I see walks with the bases loaded. I see fly balls dropped. I see grounders going through legs. I see a horrible, horrible scoreboard. It says Raiders eighteen, Sluggers three. It says Bluesox seventeen, Sluggers five. It says—"

"Stop it, Little Spirit," Rachel said. "We don't want to hear about the past anymore. Let's get serious here for a second."

"Serious about what?" Zach said, changing his voice.

"Like you said before, we're heading into opening day. Can you really picture us—the Southside Sluggers—as a winning team? I mean—come on!"

2 Opening Day

"Welcome to Opening Day," Commissioner Brady said into the microphone.

It was a perfect day for baseball. The sun was shining. The flags in the outfield were fluttering. The Sluggers sat together in their green-and-orange game uniforms listening to the commissioner's annual speech.

Afterward, the Sluggers were playing against their arch-rivals, the Mudsharks. They weren't the best team in the league, but they were a challenge for the Sluggers. And they got special pleasure out of making the Southside Sluggers look, and feel, bad.

"I have two announcements to make," the commissioner said. "First, I am retiring at the end of this year as commissioner of the Lotus Pines Youth Baseball League."

A murmur went up through the crowd.

"Second," the commissioner said, "I've decided to show my appreciation for all you have given me. Copies of three rare and valuable baseball cards in my collection have already been hidden—somewhere in Bloom Field Park. The challenge for all Youth League kids—using clues I will provide for *you*—is to find them. This means no advice or interference by parents. Then, the winning *kids* can swap their copies for the real cards."

"Holy cow!" Rachel said.

Zach and Andy jabbed each other in the ribs.

"You have two weeks," the commissioner continued, "until the end of the Sluggers–Mudsharks next game on the Saturday after next. The Great Lotus Pines Baseball Card Hunt will then conclude with the presentation of the three rare cards."

Commissioner Brady talked about how the hunt would work. After today's game, each player would receive a copy of *The Youth Baseball League Rule Book*. Inside the rule book would be a sheet of paper. Four riddles would be printed on it. Each would lead to the location of a clue. The players would then use all four clues to find where the cards were hidden.

"Oh, one more thing," the commissioner said. None of the clues will be on the playing field. I want to repeat that. *None* of the clues will be found on the baseball field itself. So confine your search for clues to the rest of the park."

With that, the umpires motioned the teams to enter the field. The Sluggers clambered down the stands and met up with Coach Terwilliger.

"Wait right here," he said. "I'll go get the equipment."

While they waited everyone talked about the Great Baseball Card Hunt. Only Seth Bradigan stood off to the side.

"Where do you think those cards are?" said Zach excitedly.

"I don't know," said Rachel. "But they're somewhere in the park. And we can eliminate the field when we search for clues. The commissioner was clear about that."

"Yeah," Andy said. "But who do you think the three cards could be?"

Everyone had an opinion.

Rachel Langlin had more than just an opinion.

"I don't know about the other two," she said. "But I hope one of 'em is Darryl Strawberry."

"Impossible," Zach said.

"He's right," a voice from a few feet away added. "It can't be Darryl Strawberry."

Rachel turned and squinted her eyes. It was Seth.

"Why not?" she asked.

"Simple," Seth said. "The commissioner said the cards are rare. Darryl Strawberry's still playing, so most of his cards aren't rare enough—even his old New York Mets cards. There are plenty of Darryl Strawberry cards around. I've even got some."

Rachel's face turned as red as her hair. "But you don't have his 'first traded' card from nineteen eighty-three," Rachel replied. "That's pretty rare now."

"But not as rare as the kind of cards the commissioner is probably talking about," said Seth.

Rachel was about to say something more when the

coach came back with a duffel bag full of bats and balls. "Warm up, everybody!" he said.

A new season was about to begin.

The team scattered, leaving Rachel and Seth standing face to face. Then Seth slowly walked away.

"Play ball!" the umpire cried.

The Sluggers took their places on the field with Andy behind the plate and Zach on the mound.

Lisa Choi led off for the Mudsharks. Andy recognized her from last year. She was a "touch" hitter who usually flicked her bat out. She just aimed to punch the ball over the infield.

"Move in!" Andy yelled to his outfielders.

Rachel in right field and Susan Stein in center took a few steps forward. In left, Seth Bradigan came way in.

"That's too much!" Andy cried. But Seth wouldn't listen. "Oh well," Andy muttered to himself. "He'll have to learn the hard way."

As Zach wound up for his first pitch the chant went up: "Hey batter, hey batter, hey batter . . . *swing!*"

"Stee-rike one!" the umpire barked.

The season was under way!

After another strike Andy called for Zach to "waste one." He figured a nervous batter with two quick strikes on her just might go for a really bad pitch.

The pitch came in high and away. But Lisa reached out with an awkward chopping swing—and somehow hit the ball! A high drive went shooting out to center, over Susan Stein's head. She turned and ran. Andy could have kicked himself for moving her in so far.

The ball kept sailing and Susan kept running. There was no chance. Then Andy heard a voice.

It sounded like "Clear out!" But there was no way Seth Bradigan could reach this ball. It was too deep—and Seth had too far to go.

But then Andy heard it again, "Clear out!"

Seth came speeding across the field and stretched for the ball. It plunked in his glove—and stuck!

"Yer o-o-o-u-u-t!" the umpire roared.

"Well, I'll be!" Andy cried.

The astonished Mudshark batter was already at second base by now. She stood frozen in disbelief.

In right field Rachel was also just standing there. "Is this guy for real?" she asked herself.

The magic of Seth's catch wore off quickly. The next Mudshark batter hit a high pop-up to shortstop Ernie Peters.

"Clear out! Clear out!"

Seth's battle cry filled the air again. He charged straight in from left field. Ernie ducked down to get out of his way.

Seth lunged over the crouching shortstop and almost made a diving, circus catch. But the ball brushed the webbing of his glove and trickled in toward the pitcher's mound. The batter wound up on second base.

"What was that?" Ernie asked, as he stood up and brushed himself off.

"I almost made another one of my great catches," answered Seth.

"Yeah, but if you had stayed in left—where you

belong—I would have caught the pop-up for an easy out."

Seth's blunder helped to get the Mudsharks rolling. They went on to score five runs in the top of the first inning.

Andy, Rachel, and Zach sat next to each other in the dugout. They avoided talking about the big Mudsharks lead. Instead, they made plans for the baseball card hunt.

"Let's work on this hunt together," Zach suggested. "What do you say, Sherlock?"

The kids often referred to Rachel as "Sherlock." She had a great knack for solving mysteries—just like the famous detective from fiction, Sherlock Holmes.

"Sure, I'm game!" Rachel answered. "How about you, Andy?"

"Count me in. And let's ask Seth to join us too."

"That ball hog?" barked Rachel. "He'll just try to take over."

"C'mon," Andy said. "Let's give him a chance."

Seth overheard the conversation and slid over to them.

"I'd like to help you guys out, but I work better alone."

"So we noticed," muttered Rachel as she grabbed a bat and climbed out of the dugout.

Rachel blooped a single to left. Marty Franklin then doubled to center field. This put runners on second and third. Seth Bradigan came walking up to the plate.

"Hey, Seth!" Andy called from the bench. "Knock 'em home!"

On the first pitch Seth really powdered one. He hit the ball so hard it was still rising when it cleared the home-run fence 200 feet down the first-base line.

The Sluggers bench exploded.

"Three runs!" Andy cried. "What a shot!"

"I think I'm going to faint," Zach smiled.

"*Foul ball!*" the umpire cried.

"Now I'm really going to faint," Zach said.

The Mudsharks' manager came out to talk to his pitcher. When play resumed Seth Bradigan was being walked intentionally.

"Boo!" the Sluggers cried from the bench. "No fair!"

"Hey, cut that out," Coach Terwilliger said. "There's no law against an intentional walk. It's good strategy. And, anyhow, it will give us bases loaded with no outs."

The Mudsharks' catcher—Chip Hoover—stood and motioned for another high, outside pitch.

"Ball three!" called the umpire.

The next pitch came in high and outside again. But Seth refused to be walked. He took a giant step across the plate and hit the ball to shallow left field. Seth's shot was caught. The base runners couldn't advance. And the Sluggers now had one out.

Michelle Brooks, the next batter, quickly went to a three-ball, two-strike count.

"Concentration!" the coach called out.

"Cream one, Michelle!" Rachel cried from third.

The next pitch was ladled in over the plate. Michelle swung and hit the ball—straight into the first baseman's glove.

"Some Sluggers!" the Mudsharks' third baseman yelled out. "Maybe we ought to call you the Southside *Flubbers* instead."

Seth's refusal to be walked and Michelle's easy out had killed the Sluggers' rally. At the end of the inning, the score was still 5–0.

"Now all we need to do is hold 'em," Andy said, walking Zach out to the pitcher's mound. "Then we can score some runs and make this thing close."

"Sure," Zach replied, "I'll keep it close."

But the Southside Sluggers never got any closer than 5–0. Zach was replaced by relief pitcher Robin Hayes after three innings. And by the end of the fifth inning, the Sluggers were down 9–0.

The first two Mudsharks batters in the sixth hit easy ground balls. The Sluggers messed up on both of them. Second baseman Luis Diaz threw over Marty's head at first base. Then, on the next play, Marty's foot came off the bag when he took the throw from shortstop Ernie Peters.

"Time-out!" Andy yelled. Robin and the other infielders met the catcher at the mound for a talk.

"We're jinxed," Andy sighed.

"We're not jinxed," Robin said.

"Get a grip on yourself," an unfamiliar voice chimed in.

"Seth!" Luis cried. "What are *you* doing here? Out-

fielders aren't supposed to come to a talk on the mound! Don't you know anything?"

Seth's eyes were cool as steel. "I know more than anyone here. I just thought you guys could use a little extra advice."

Lisa Choi was up next. Rachel moved in, but only a step. She remembered that rocket Lisa had hit in the first.

Robin quickly got two strikes on the batter. This time, instead of another wasted pitch, Andy called for one right down the middle. He figured the best way to fool Lisa was to give her an unexpected good pitch—instead of a bad one.

Lisa swung and hit a lazy fly to center. Susan Stein ran easily toward it.

"I got it!" Susan cried. And then she saw a body streaking in from left field.

"Clear out!"

There it was again, like a foghorn.

"Clear out! Clear out!"

"Uh-oh!" Susan shouted, freezing in her tracks. "It's Clear Out Bradigan!"

Seth slowed up at that moment—not wanting to plow into the statue in front of him. The ball fell between them.

"Clear Out Bradigan," repeated Rachel as she scooped up the ball and threw it to second base. "Clear Out Bradigan! There's a nickname that will stick."

The final score was Mudsharks 12, Sluggers 5. "You

guys showed heart out there today," Coach Terwilliger said, trying to look on the bright side.

"We were terrible early on," Zach said with a faint smile. "But we did score five late runs. We only lost by seven runs."

"Seven runs, twelve runs, or one run in extra innings," Seth snapped. "I hate to lose!"

After the field was cleared, three large boxes were brought out. Each player in the league lined up to get an official rule book from the commissioner's office. They were all eager to get a first look at the riddles—and begin the hunt.

Andy noticed Seth on line behind him.

"You sure you don't want to team up with us?" he asked.

"Thanks, but I can find the cards on my own," bragged Seth. "They'll make a great addition to *my* already great baseball card collection."

3 Park Full of Clues

Rachel, Zach, and Andy walked over to their favorite spot, the big oak tree on the third-base side of the field. They tossed their gloves in a pile, plopped down under the tree, and cracked open their root beers.

Rachel took her riddle sheet out of the rule book. Andy and Zach also looked over their riddle sheets.

"I think I figured out riddle number three," Zach said. "The clue's at the drinking fountain."

"Not so fast," Andy said. "I think riddle two points to the parking lot. What do you think, Rachel?"

"I think we're doing this all wrong," Rachel said. "I think we have to think things out before we run off."

"What?" Zach exclaimed, "and let everyone else out there beat us to the punch?"

"You mean like them?" Rachel asked, looking around.

The park was alive with Youth Leaguers going wild. Luis Diaz and Michelle Brooks were crawling under grandstand seats. Marty Franklin and Susan Stein were peering into a drainpipe. And Ernie Peters was scrambling up a fence.

What's more, Rachel saw several Mudsharks searching under garbage cans, and two Tigers trying to move a huge rock. Kids were shouting, climbing, and running in every direction.

"Come on, Rach," Andy said. "Let's go check out the parking lot."

"And the drinking fountain," Zach said.

"You guys do what you like," Rachel said. "I'll be right here. Thinking."

With that, Zach and Andy took off. Rachel leaned back against the tree. *You had to solve a mystery one step at a time*, she thought. *You had to have a plan.*

She looked around. In the whole park, she saw only one person who wasn't running after something. Seth Bradigan was sitting four trees down. He wasn't studying his riddle sheet, either. He was just sitting there with his eyes closed.

Several minutes later, Zach and Andy returned.

"Nothing," Zach said. "No clues in the parking lot."

"And none at the drinking fountain," added Andy.

"Okay," Rachel said. "Now we can get organized. We're in this together, aren't we?"

"You're right," Andy said. "Remember our pact. If any of us finds a baseball card, it belongs to all three of us."

"Well, I know what I'm doing with my share of the cards," Zach announced. "I'm gonna trade my card for a twelve-speed mountain bike."

Andy's mouth dropped open in shock. "Do you mean you'd trade a rare baseball card for a twelve-speed bike!"

"Well, okay," Zach said. "Maybe not a twelve-speed. Maybe only a three-speed."

"You don't get it, do you?" Andy continued. "These cards aren't for trading. They're for keeping. No kid in Lotus Pines has cards this good."

"So?" Zach said.

Andy threw up his hands. "You'll never understand collecting baseball cards."

"It's like collecting history," Rachel said.

Zach grinned. "Collecting history, eh? I'll give you two Abe Lincolns for a John F. Kennedy and three Florence Nightingales."

Andy rolled his eyes. "Not regular history—*baseball* history. You hold those old cards in your hand and you can just *feel* what it was like back then. Ty Cobb rounding third. Babe Ruth swatting a home run over Yankee Stadium."

"Darryl Strawberry," Rachel added, "gunning down a runner from deep in the outfield."

"All right, all right," Zach said. "I get the picture. Can we go back to the riddles now?"

"With pleasure," Rachel said. "Andy, why don't you read Riddle One out loud."

"Ahem," Andy began.

"Home game, away game,
Day game, night game
Rain, snow, or thunder.
There's one kind of roof
All baseball games play under.

"Look through three dozen leaves
And it's right in your hand.
Count a score of two for the clue.
Is there a chance you'll understand?"

Rachel took a long drink of her root beer.

"Got any ideas, Zach?"

"I don't know about you two, but I'm lost."

"Andy?"

"I'd say under a roof. Except we don't play under a roof, so I don't get it. What about you, Rachel. You're the Sherlock Holmes here. What do you think?"

"I think maybe you're on to something with the roof. You know that shed out there—out past left field? Doesn't Mr. Clancy, the groundskeeper, store up big bags of leaves out there under that roof?"

"You're right!" Andy said. "Those bags must have a lot more than three dozen leaves. And they're under the roof."

"Come on," Zach said. "Let's get out there." Then he looked at Rachel. "*Now* what's wrong?"

"I think we should think about this a little bit longer," she said.

Fifteen minutes later, three heads peered into a small

window of the maintenance shed. There were several large brown bags lying on the floor.

"Too bad it's locked," Andy said.

"Too bad we don't have the key," Zach added.

"I don't think this is it," Rachel said.

"Of course it is," Zach replied. "Big bags of leaves. A roof. It's perfect."

Rachel shook her head. "Uh-uh. I don't think the commissioner would have left a clue locked inside a shed. How would he expect us to get in?"

"Don't be ridiculous," Zach said. "For one thing we could pick the lock . . ."

"We don't know how to pick locks," Andy said. "Besides, it's against the law."

"Well," Zach said. "We could use the key, then."

"Except we don't have a key."

"We don't need one. Look who's coming."

"Mr. Clancy!" the three of them cried.

After a long and confusing explanation, Mr. Clancy just told them he was sorry.

"I can open the door for you," he said, "but it won't do any good. Those bags are full of fertilizer. We burned the leaves last fall."

"Good try, Sis," Zach said, as the three of them glumly marched back to the oak tree.

"You can't expect to find every clue the first time," Andy said.

"You know what gets me," Rachel said, pointing to a lonely figure several trees down. "That Clear Out Bradigan. What's he *doing* over there all by himself, anyway? Why isn't he running around looking for clues?"

"Why don't we go ask him?" Andy said.

The three of them walked over to the tree where Seth was sitting, reading his rule book. "Hey, Seth," Andy asked, "got any ideas about this first riddle here?"

"I don't need any ideas," Seth said.

"Why not?"

"Because I've already solved it," Seth answered.

The three Sluggers' jaws dropped.

"What do you mean you solved it?" Rachel said. "You've been sitting under this tree for the past half hour. How could you solve it?"

"I'm telling you," Seth said. "I solved the riddle."

"Okay. Then what's it mean? Where's the clue?"

Seth laughed. "What do you think I am—dumb? This is supposed to be a contest."

"It's a baseball card hunt."

"Well—whatever. The way I see it, it's every kid for himself."

Rachel sighed. "You know what, Seth? You hunt baseball cards the same way you play baseball."

"Oh, and I suppose you don't think I'm any good at baseball either," Seth snapped.

"Not at all," Rachel said. "You're good, Seth. In fact, you're better than good. At least you could be."

Seth's eyes narrowed. "What do you mean—could be?"

"I mean there's more to playing baseball than just trying to make great plays all the time."

"Oh yeah? Like what?"

"I don't know," Rachel said. "Like being a team. We might have *won* that game today—if you'd just stopped trying to be a hero out there on every play."

"The way I see it, without me we lose that game by about eighteen runs instead of just seven."

This was true, perhaps, but there was no way Rachel was going to admit it. Andy stepped in to cool things down.

"Anyway, Seth," he said. "If you feel like working on some of the other riddles—"

"Maybe some other time," Seth said. "I gotta get going right now. Okay?"

Seth picked up his glove, shoes, and rule book.

"See you at practice," Andy said.

"Right," Seth said, mounting his bike. Then he turned to Rachel with a strange look in his eyes. "Teamwork," he said. "You want some teamwork? How's this: A *leaf* can also be a *page*."

"Huh?" Rachel said. "What d'you mean?"

Before she could ask again, Seth was riding away.

"What was that all about?" Andy asked.

"I'm not sure," Rachel said. "Come on, you two. Let's get going."

Late that night Rachel suddenly jumped out of bed and ran to Zach's room. "Wake up," she said, shaking him. "Listen." Then she read the first riddle aloud:

> "*Home game, away game,*
> *Day game, night game*
> *Rain, snow, or thunder.*

There's one kind of roof
All baseball games play under."

"So?" Zach said. "Sounds like the first riddle."
"Keep listening:

> "*Look through three dozen leaves*
> *And it's right in your hand.*
> *Count a score of two for the clue.*
> *Is there a chance you'll understand?*"

"You're right. That is the first riddle," Zach said. "Now can I go back to sleep?"

"No! Now try this: 'A leaf can also be a page.'"

"Okay. Maybe it can."

"Not maybe. It *is*. That's what Seth told us today: *A leaf can also be a page.*"

"Is that all?"

"What do you mean, Is that all? Don't you see it? It's a book! The riddle is about a book! It has pages and you're holding it right in your hand."

"That's great," Zach said. "Except we still have one problem. Most books we read have at least three dozen pages. So, which book is it?"

"H-m-m," Rachel said. She plopped down on the carpet, holding the riddle sheet in front of her eyes.

"At least we know it's on page thirty-six," said Zach.

"Huh? How do you get page thirty-six?" asked Rachel, not really thinking.

"Easy. Every dozen I know is twelve. And twelve times three is thirty-six."

"Good, Zach!"

"Yeah, I know. Now can I go back to sleep?"

"Okay."

Rachel went back into her room. A moment later Zach's head peeped around the corner.

"It's the fortieth word on the page," he said.

"How do you know?" Rachel asked.

"Listen to this line from the riddle," Zach said. " 'Count a *score* of two for the clue.' "

"So?"

"So, *score* is an old word meaning twenty," said Zach. "So, a 'score of two' equals twenty times two— or forty."

"How come I didn't think of that?" Rachel asked.

"I don't know," Zach shrugged. "You're good at words. And I guess I'm good at numbers. Good night, Sis."

"Good night, Zach."

Rachel got back into bed. Now she knew the clue was the fortieth word of the thirty-sixth page of a book. But she had to discover *what* book.

It made sense that it would be a baseball book. But what was this business about the roof? What does a roof have to do with a book? These questions kept swirling around in Rachel's head as she finally dropped off to sleep.

Meanwhile, several blocks away, Seth Bradigan clicked on a flashlight. He reached in the drawer next to his bed and pulled out a book.

He knew it was the book that fit Riddle Number One. It contained the first clue to the cards.

He turned to page 36 and counted out forty words. He knew what the clue word was. The hard part was figuring out what the clue meant.

This was the question on Seth's mind as he folded the riddle paper and put it back in the book. He put the book back in the drawer. Then he clicked off the flashlight and went to sleep.

On Monday, the first day of spring vacation, Rachel and Zach got up late. There was no school for two whole weeks.

Mr. Langlin was dressed in his Southside Ice Cream Shop uniform. "Come on, you two," he said to Rachel and Zach. "I'll give you a ride to practice."

On the way they picked up Andy. All three friends sat in the backseat together.

"What's going on back there?" Mr. Langlin asked. "It's not like you to be so quiet."

"Oh, we're not quiet," Zach said. "We're thinking."

"About what?"

"The baseball card hunt. We'd like to let you in on it, Dad, but under the rules, I don't think we can."

Suddenly Rachel bolted up in the backseat. "You've done it again, Zach!"

"I have?" Zach replied.

"Don't you see? All baseball games are played *under the rules*. Home games, away games, day games, night games, in any kind of weather. All games are played under the same roof—under the same baseball rules."

"So, it's the rule book!" Andy shouted.

All three Sluggers scrambled through their backpacks to find their rule books.

They turned to page 36.

And counted out forty words.

"*Chance?*" Zach said.

And together the three of them cried:

"*Chance!*"

The sentence in *The Youth Baseball League Rule Book* read like this: "Every player must be given at least one *chance* at bat in each game."

But what did the clue "chance" mean?

4 Practice Makes Perfect

Coach Terwilliger took a stick and drew a baseball diamond in the dirt. "I was a little disappointed with the Mudsharks game," he said. "Not just that we lost. But the way we covered the field." The coach picked up an acorn.

"Now suppose this acorn is the shortstop." He put the acorn in the shortstop's spot on the diamond.

"And this bottle cap is the center fielder. Now here comes a fly ball." The coach drew a curved line in the dirt. It showed the ball sailing over second base into shallow center field.

"Whose call is it—Bottle Cap's, or Acorn's?"

"It's Acorn's ball," Marty Franklin said. "It belongs to the shortstop."

"Why?"

"Because he's closer."

The coach shook his head. "Neither player was closer," he said. "So who should call it—Bottle Cap or Acorn?"

"That's easy," Rachel said. "Whoever yells loudest."

"Wrong," the coach said. "Bottle Cap was running *in* on the ball. So she had a better view of the play. The player with the better view always makes the call."

"What happens if nobody's running in or out?" Seth asked.

"Good question," the coach said. He drew a ball headed between left and center field.

Then he searched through the grass. "Anyone see another acorn? I need a left fielder."

"How about a hot dog?" Rachel suggested. Everyone laughed except Seth.

The coach said that a play like this could belong to either outfielder. The general rule was that the outfielder with the best view of the ball should make the call. But, above all, players needed to respect each other's turf.

"You got that, Acorn?" the coach said to shortstop Ernie Peters.

"Respect," Ernie said, with a smile on his face.

"How about you, Bottle Cap?"

"Right, Coach," Susan Stein said. "Respect."

Then the coach paused, looking straight at Seth Bradigan for a moment.

"As for the rest of you Bottle Caps and Acorns— that's enough talk. Let's get to work!"

Andy and Rachel watched Ernie Peters take batting practice. The coach was lobbing in pitches. Ernie hit a line drive to the gap in the outfield.

"Nice shot, Ernie!" Andy cried.

Rachel reached in her back pocket and took out the riddle sheet. "While we're waiting—" she said.

"I've gotta work on my swing," Andy said. He took an imaginary slow-motion swing at an imaginary pitch.

"Your swing is fine," Rachel said. "What about Riddle Number Two?"

"We never even solved Riddle Number One yet."

"Sure we did. *Chance.*"

"What's chance?" Andy asked.

"Chance is chance. The chance to have a turn at bat. The chance to solve the next riddle. I don't know."

The coach's pitches came in a little faster. Ernie fouled one off. Then he hit a weak grounder.

"Good rip, Ernie," the coach said. "Keep your head down. That's it."

They watched as the speed of the coach's pitches increased. Ernie kept battling—trying to make contact.

"Ever notice something about batting practice?" Rachel said. "At first the pitches come in nice and fat. Then it gets harder and harder."

"So?"

"So that's what I figure these riddles are like, too. At first the commissioner just lobs them in at us. Then they get harder and harder."

"You call that first clue a lob? I thought it was really tough. And we still don't know what it means."

Rachel watched Ernie hit a one-hopper to second.

"Put it this way," Rachel said. "I think the riddles are going to be the easy part. The tough part'll be figuring out what the clues mean and putting them together."

The coach signaled for one more pitch. Ernie swung and stroked a clean single to center.

"Nice job, Ernie," the coach said. "Next!"

Andy grabbed his bat and headed to home plate.

While Andy took his swings, Rachel unfolded her riddle sheet and read slowly:

There once was a silver-topped Ford
Who was proud of the runs that he scored
With the game on the line in the very last inning
He gave out a sign that the home team was winning
And that's where the secret was stored.

"H-m-m," Rachel said to herself. She could see why Zach might have thought this riddle was about the parking lot. A Ford was a car. And the parking lot was the only place in the park that cars were allowed.

She watched Andy take a huge swing at a fastball.

"Ease up!" the coach shouted. "Stop trying to kill the ball."

This was Andy's main batting problem—trying to knock every pitch out of the park. The trouble was that sometimes he *would* get hold of one and send it flying. Then he'd swing even harder the next time. And miss.

Rachel wondered if she wasn't doing the same thing with the riddle—trying to solve the whole thing in one swipe. If only she had a hint of where to start.

On the next swing Andy provided her with that hint. The pitch came in right down the middle. The ball shot over Seth Bradigan's head, cleared the fence—and bounced off the scoreboard in left center.

The scoreboard was the old-fashioned kind. Instead of being electric, it had square holes for each inning. The holes were covered by wooden flaps. After every half inning the official scorekeeper—Mr. Clancy—would pull in a flap toward him. Then he would put up a big wooden card with a number on it to show how many runs the team had scored.

Andy's hit made a loud thump as it smashed into the scoreboard. Rachel watched Seth pick up the ball and throw it in. But instead of going back to his position, Seth studied the wooden flap where the ball hit. He reached into his back pocket and took out a piece of paper. Seth read something on the paper, looked back at the scoreboard, then back at the paper again.

"The riddle!" gasped Rachel. "The scoreboard had something to do with the second riddle!"

"Why the second riddle?" Zach asked after practice was over and the three of them were collecting their gear. "Why not the third—or the fourth?"

"Clear Out Bradigan may not be so bright *on* the field," Rachel said, "but *off* the field he knows what he's doing. He's working on this thing the same way we are—one clue at a time."

"How do we know he hasn't already solved Riddle Two?"

"We don't," Andy said.

"Good," Zach said. "Then let's hit the road. I want to get back home and play some Retro Blast."

Rachel held out her hand. "Hold on a second. You can play video games any old time, Zach. Let's go check out that scoreboard."

Zach looked at Andy, who shrugged.

"All right," Zach said. "Let's get it over with."

On the way over, Zach announced that he knew of at least three good reasons why the clue wasn't on the scoreboard.

"Name one," Rachel said.

"It's too obvious."

"So?"

"Kids were crawling all over that scoreboard on the first day," Zach pointed out. "And nobody found a thing."

"Okay, that's one good reason," said Rachel. "Name another."

"The riddle's about a car. A Ford with a silver top. I don't see any cars on the scoreboard."

"What about all the ads?"

She pointed to the billboards for local products that were painted under the scoreboard. Munchies Bakery. Lotus Diner. Walt's Ice Cubes. Sneakerama Sneakers. Mr. Langlin was even thinking of having a sign for the Southside Ice Cream Shop.

"See?" Zach said, after they had probed the entire length of the scoreboard. "No car ads. No silver-topped cars. No nothing."

"Huh?" Rachel couldn't hear what Zach was saying. She had climbed up onto the scoreboard. She was half-in, half-out of the fourth-inning hole. Andy was holding her by the feet so she could see in.

"Nothing," she said, when he pulled her back up. Her face was smudged. Her hair looked funny from being upside down.

"I told you there's no clue in that old scoreboard," said Zach.

Andy took out his riddle sheet. "Hey, Rach," he said after a minute. "What does *the game on the line* mean to you?"

"It means the clutch moment—the tough part of the game," Rachel said. "Why?"

Andy pulled at his lip, deep in thought. "Or maybe *a game on the line* is how a game appears on a scoreboard—a bunch of numbers, all lined up."

"But we already know it's not the scoreboard," Zach said. "Otherwise, we would've found something."

"Well, hold on a minute," Andy said. "What if the silver-topped Ford is a man instead of a car?"

"How could a Ford be a man?" asked Zach.

"Simple! It's a man's name," replied Andy.

"Like Ford Frick, ex-president of the American League," Rachel said. "What're you getting at, Andy?"

"There are lots of Fords—car inventor Henry Ford, President Gerald Ford, and the great pitcher Whitey Ford. You name it. All we need to do is find a Ford with silver hair—the silver top—that fits the rest of the clue."

Suddenly a gray head wearing a baseball cap popped out of the hole for the top half of the third inning.

"Did someone mention the name Ford?" it said.

"Mr. Clancy! What're you doing here?"

Mr. Clancy chuckled. "I'm the scoreboard keeper, remember? What're you kids doing here? Oh, wait—the card hunt, right? You're snoopin' around."

"You got us," Zach said. "Well, that's enough snooping, right, gang? We better get going now."

"Wait! Come back a minute." The three Sluggers stopped. "You're the second ones snoopin' around here askin' about the name Ford. What is it about Ford? It's not such a bad name, you know."

"Is y-your name Ford?" Rachel asked.

Mr. Clancy nodded sheepishly.

"I thought your name was Fred," Zach said.

"It is," Mr. Clancy said. "Er, well—sort of. When I was a kid I thought Ford sounded too fancy. So I called myself Fred. But now I've been thinking about goin' back to Ford again. Sounds classy—don't you think? Ford Clancy."

"Mr. Clancy," Rachel said, "I can't tell you how much you've helped us here."

"I have?" Mr. Clancy said.

"You bet," Rachel said. "Well, we've got to get going now. Oh, one more thing. You said someone else was snooping around asking about the name Ford?"

Mr. Clancy nodded. "Good-lookin' fella. Wait! Same uniform as you three. You must be teammates, eh?"

"You can say that again," Rachel said. And with that, the three Sluggers took off.

* * *

On Thursday Zach, Andy, and Rachel went to Bloom Field. Rachel insisted that they see the game between the Mudsharks and the Bluesox.

"I still don't get this," Zach said, as they climbed up the stands. A Pony League game, for the older kids, was just ending on the field.

"You don't have to get it," Rachel said. "Just be awake until the last inning and I'll show you."

"Look who's here," Andy said.

It was Seth Bradigan.

"I swear," Andy said. "That guy's following us."

"He's not following us," Rachel said. "He's just following the same clues as we are."

Seth walked up to them with a big grin on his face.

"Hi, everybody. Workin' on those riddles?"

"Sure are," Andy said. "How 'bout you?"

Seth blew on his hand and rubbed his chest to show how proud he was.

"Just solved Riddle Number Two."

"No fooling," Rachel said. "Find a good clue during that Pony League game?"

"How'd you ever guess?" replied Seth.

"Oh, I don't know. Just lucky, I suppose," smiled Rachel.

"Never hurts to be lucky," Seth said. "Well, that's it for me. I'll see you three at the game tomorrow."

"Right," Rachel said.

And then, as he walked away, she muttered under her breath, "Seth's luck might not be as good as he thinks. It's just possible that Clear Out Bradigan came up with the wrong clue!"

5 The Kismet Kid

"What are you talking about?" Andy asked. "What makes you think that Seth might have the wrong clue?"

Rachel stared at the scoreboard before she answered. "That was a Pony League game they were playing down there! Pony League plays nine innings. We only play six!"

"I don't get it," Andy said. "Do you get it, Zach?"

"I don't even know what we're doing here," Zach said.

"How many times do I need to explain it?" Rachel said. "It's in the riddle: *A silver-topped Ford*—that's Mr. Clancy. He's *proud of the runs that he scored*—those are the scoreboard runs. *The game on the line in the very last inning.* Those are the numbers on the scoreboard."

"Somehow I get the feeling I've heard all this before," Zach said. "How about you, Andy?"

Andy threw up his hands.

"Don't you see it?" Rachel said. "During the last inning Mr. Clancy does something—but only when the *home team was winning. That's where the secret was stored.*"

"But what does he do?" asked Zach. "And why does he only do it during the last inning—when the home team is ahead?"

A man in a Mudsharks jacket two rows down suddenly started yelling, "Let's go, Mudsharks! Let's go, Mudsharks!" The game was about to start.

"Well?" Zach said. "What *does* happen in the last inning?"

"Sh-h-h!" Rachel said. "We'll talk about it later."

The Bluesox began the game with three straight outs. First there was a pop-up to the shortstop. Then a quick strikeout. And finally an easy grounder to the pitcher.

Lisa Choi of the Mudsharks was the lead-off batter in the bottom of the first. Andy remembered her hitting style from last week. She was the one who got the big hit in the last inning. The one who liked high pitches.

Then it dawned on Andy. Today, the Mudsharks might not even *need* a last inning. As the home team, if they were ahead, they didn't bat in the last inning!

That's what the riddle was talking about! Mr. Clancy wouldn't put *any number* on the scoreboard for the bottom of the sixth—if the home team was winning.

He leaned over and whispered his discovery to Rachel and Zach.

"Exactly!" Rachel cried. "But maybe Mr. Clancy does something with the scoreboard—instead of putting up a final number."

"Like what?" Zach asked.

"I don't know," Rachel said. "But, whatever it is, Seth just might have gotten it wrong. He was watching a Pony League game. They play nine innings instead of six."

"But the home team was ahead in the last inning of the Pony League game," Andy chimed in. "And the last inning is the last inning. Mr. Clancy would do the same thing for the ninth inning of a Pony League game as he would for the sixth inning of a Youth League game."

"Yeah," Rachel replied. "But he would be doing it to a different place on the scoreboard."

In the bottom of the fifth inning, good old Lisa was up with two on and the score tied at 1–1. It had been a real pitcher's duel so far.

"Come on!" Zach yelled. If Lisa didn't get a hit, the home-team Mudsharks would need to bat in the last inning. Crazy as it seemed, they had to root for the Mudsharks to get a run and win the game.

"Give her a high pitch!" Andy cried.

A man in a Mudsharks jacket scowled.

"That's my daughter down there. How dare you call for a high pitch!"

"I'm on your side," Andy said, shaking his head at the thought. "She *likes* high pitches!"

* * *

The next pitch was a high one. Lisa slammed it into left field. Two runs scored. By the end of the fifth inning, the Mudsharks were ahead by 7. And the Sluggers in the stands were both relieved and annoyed.

"Now all we need to do is wait," Rachel said. "What a price to pay to get a clue—rooting for those Mudsharks!"

So they waited. They kept their eyes glued to the scoreboard. The first Bluesox of the inning struck out. The second batter popped up for another out.

"I don't see anything," Zach said. "Do you see anything?"

Rachel was about to say no. But suddenly Mr. Clancy's head popped out of the hole that was used for scoring the bottom of the sixth.

"Of course!" Rachel cried. "He always sticks his head out when he's pretty sure the game's over. But what does that mean?"

"The only unusual thing I see," Andy said, "is he left the flap out instead of pulling it in. He's covering up the sign for Walt's Ice Cubes."

"Walt's Ice C-U-B—-S," Zach said. "The flap's covering up the *E*."

Rachel pulled out Zach's hand and slapped him a high five. "That's it!" she said.

"What's it? Walt's Ice Cubs?" Zach asked with a puzzled look on his face.

"No! Just Cubs," Rachel laughed. "The Chicago Cubs baseball team. You get it?"

Andy gave Rachel a big thumbs up. "Two clues down—two more to go. You're great, Rachel."

"We're all great!" yelled Zach. "Now all we have to do is figure out—what *about* the Cubs."

"Poor Seth!" Rachel said suddenly with a broad smile. "The flap for the bottom of the ninth inning covers the first 'S' in the 'Sneakerama' sign. He must be going wild trying to figure out what 'neakerama' could possibly mean."

"Yeah," Andy said. "And while Seth wrestles with 'neakerama' we'll zero in on the Cubs and Chance. Two great clues!"

The next morning, all the way to the Langlin house Andy repeated to himself, "Chance, Cubs. Cubs, Chance. Chance, Cubs . . ."

It was game day. The Sluggers were playing the Tigers. Andy found Rachel and Zach in the front yard playing catch with their uniforms on.

"Just warming up today's pitcher," Rachel said.

Zach's fastball popped into her glove.

"How's it going?" Andy said to Zach. "You nervous about the game?"

"No sense being nervous," Rachel said. "Whatever happens, happens. It's Kismet."

"It's what?" Andy asked.

"Kismet," Zach echoed, looking straight at Andy.

"You kiss yourself," Andy said. "I'm not kissing anybody."

"Not *kiss*," Rachel said. "Kismet. I found it in the dictionary when I was looking up *chance*. It means fate, destiny. Whatever happens, happens."

"You know what I hope happens?" Andy said.

"What?" Zach asked.

"I hope we play like a *real* team today and beat the Tigers."

"For us to beat the Tigers," said Rachel, "we'd have to play like some *other* team."

Zach laughed and stared into his baseball, as if it were a crystal ball. "The crystal ball says we will play like World Series champions today."

Zach's crystal ball couldn't have been more wrong.

In the first inning, Michelle Brooks went back behind third base for a pop-up in foul territory.

"Clear out!" she heard Seth cry.

Every Slugger tightened up and waited for the crash. Michelle kept going back, but she stopped short when she heard Seth yell again. "Clear out!"

Seth tried to make a barehand catch as the ball fell about six inches behind Michelle. Instead of an easy out, the batter had another chance. On the mound, Zach curled his tongue over his lips and popped an angry bubble-gum bubble.

"What're you doing, Michelle?" he screamed. "That was your ball!"

Michelle shot back a dirty look. "I'm respecting other people's turf—like the coach said. Remember? And I'm avoiding collisions."

Zach rolled his eyes and popped another bubble. He threw the next pitch extra hard, but it went way outside. Three more angry pitches walked the batter. One bounced in the dirt, one hit the top of the backstop, and the last was so inside, it went behind the batter.

Zach looked over to the bench. "We could've been out of this inning already if—" he began.

"Just concentrate!" the coach called out, cutting him off. But Zach had lost his concentration. He gave up three runs in the first inning.

"Kismet," Andy said walking to the dugout. "I guess it was just Kismet."

"Or Clear Out Bradigan running wild again," mumbled Rachel as she jogged by.

The Sluggers finally got something going in the third. The score was 4–0 when Luis Diaz singled. Then the Tiger pitcher got a little wild himself and walked Rachel.

When Seth came up, Coach Terwilliger flashed the "bunt" sign. It was the perfect surprise move.

"Come on, Seth!" Andy cried.

Seth rubbed some dirt on his hands. Rachel got ready to run. If things worked out, Marty Franklin would be up next with the bases loaded.

The first pitch was chest high. The perfect ball to bunt. Seth just let it go by.

"Stee-rike one!" the umpire cried.

Seth knocked some dirt off his shoes with the bat. From first, Rachel saw that the bunt sign was still on. Once again, she leaned toward second and got ready to run.

The pitch came in straight down the middle of the plate. Rachel took off—just as Seth swung with all his might.

"Whuh?" Rachel cried in total surprise.

Seth sent a screaming line drive down the first-base

line. It went right into the first baseman's mitt. The Tiger fielder then calmly walked over and stepped on first before a diving Rachel could get back to the bag. Double play. The inning was over.

From the ground, Rachel watched Seth walk toward her.

"I thought I was going to put that ball in the seats," Seth shrugged.

"You made me look bad out there," Rachel said. "Didn't you know the bunt sign was on?"

"I don't bunt," Seth said. "It would be a waste of my power."

Back at the dugout, the coach asked him, "What are you doing, Seth?"

Seth's reply was simple. "Just tryin' to win the game, Coach."

Zach Langlin got his nickname "The Tongue" by always sticking his tongue out. He did it when he was thinking, pitching, or just hanging out. But a person could actually tell how a Slugger game was going by looking at Zach Langlin's bubble-blowing.

When things went well, Zach went easy on the gum. When things started to go bad, Zach started popping bubbles. The worse things got, the more he popped. After the third inning Zach did all his gum popping from the bench. Robin Hayes came in to pitch.

In the fifth inning, things really started to pop. With runners on first and second, the Tiger batter hit a line drive to dead center field.

"Clear out!" came the cry.

"Not again," Zach moaned.

Zach watched Seth scare off Susan Stein and just miss making another *great* play. This time the ball flew right by Seth's glove and kept going deep into the outfield. Susan had to track it down back by the fence. Three runs scored.

The Sluggers' loss wasn't all Seth's fault. In the sixth inning, Ernie Peters took his extra "hippity-hop" step before throwing to first. An easy grounder became a single. Michelle backstepped away from a hard grounder at third and was off balance for the throw to second — or first. Even Rachel tried to stretch a long fly out into a double play. But her throw to third was wild and a run scored.

All the Sluggers did *something* wrong during the game. But Seth's errors were as spectacular as his occasional great plays. They were the kind of flubs that got everyone's attention. They also irritated his teammates and cost lots of runs. They were "superstar" mistakes.

The Sluggers lost the Tigers game by a whopping 16–5 score.

Afterward, Rachel wanted to get the game out of her mind. She thought about Riddle Number Three. But Zach and Andy were already on their bikes for the ride home.

"What's with Seth?" Zach said, his tongue sticking out in deep thought. "What's he trying to prove with all that 'Clear out' stuff?"

"He's not trying to prove anything," Rachel said.

"That's just him—Clear Out Bradigan. That's what he does."

Andy was chuckling as he pedaled.

"What's so funny?" Rachel asked.

"That name—'Clear Out Bradigan.' It sounds like someone on a baseball card."

"I thought you said we should go easy on the guy," Rachel said.

"We should," Andy answered. "It's just that Seth's new nickname sounds so perfect. It *is* perfect. He's Clear Out Bradigan."

"I don't see anything so perfect about him at all," bristled Rachel. "Unless you count the perfect mess he made of today's ball game."

"Hey," Andy said. "The rest of us didn't do so great either, you know. I struck out twice with runners on base."

"I guess we all have some work to do before we start winning," admitted Rachel.

"Speaking of winning," Zach said, "are we ready to get on with winning those baseball cards?"

"Yeah!" Rachel shot back. "We're bound to win them. We've got both clue number one and clue number two. Seth probably has the wrong answer to clue number two."

"We don't know for sure that Seth missed the word *Cubs* on the scoreboard," Andy said. "After all, he was smart enough to get clue number one first. Remember, he told us *leaves can be pages.*"

"I remember," Rachel said. "It just makes me think how fast we'd solve these riddles if he'd worked with us in the first place. We'd probably *have* the cards in our hands already."

"I don't understand that either," Zach said, "Why won't he work with us? What's he got to lose?"

"Plenty," Rachel said. "He's Clear Out Bradigan, remember? The one-man team. The Lone Ranger. If he starts cooperating, he won't be Clear Out Bradigan anymore. And you know what that means, don't you?"

"What?" Zach asked.

"Yeah," Andy said. "What?"

"I don't know," Rachel said. "I wonder what *would* happen if he started playing like a real teammate."

"Only Kismet will tell," Andy said.

"Yeah," Rachel said. "Kismet."

6 The Deal

Quarters jingled in Andy's pocket as he walked into the Southside Ice Cream Shop. Rachel was sitting at the counter, sipping a drink. Andy had asked both Rachel and Zach to meet him here, but Zach had to do his paper route.

"I'll have what Rachel's having," Andy told Mr. Langlin. Then he looked at the greenish sludge in Rachel's glass.

"A Pickleberry Soda," Andy groaned. "You really like that stuff?"

"I sure do," Rachel said. "I figured it might cheer me up. Did you hear? Some kids on the Rocket Raiders are already working on Riddle Four."

"Do you believe it?"

"I don't know. All I know is we're nowhere on Riddle Three."

Andy took out his riddle sheet.

"I don't want to hear it again," Rachel said. "I've read it a hundred times already this morning."

"No, listen. I got a call. From Seth Bradigan."

Rachel's blue eyes narrowed. "Oh, yeah? What does old Clear Out want now? A portable microphone—so he can shout his own name out louder?"

"He's stuck on Riddle Three," said Andy.

"Good for him. He had his chance to join us."

"He doesn't want to join us," Andy said, pausing dramatically. "He wants to trade!"

Rachel laughed out loud. "Trade? What's he going to trade?"

"Information."

"Information?"

"We tell *him* something we know," Andy explained. "And he tells us something that he knows."

Rachel shook her head back and forth.

"But we don't know anything!" she said. "Here's the whole riddle. I know it by heart.

> "*Do this to a bath*
> *And get something to hit at home.*
> *Do the opposite to a chair*
> *And get something to comb.*
>
> "*Do the same to Oscar's third friend*
> *And leave it at that.*
> *This clue is all done*
> *Do you smell the rat?*

"Except for who Oscar is," Rachel continued. "I have no idea what any of it means. I'm completely in the dark."

Andy's face was serious. "That's what I tried to tell

Seth. But he insists we *do* know something. So what d'you say?"

Rachel's shook her head again. "Forget it."

"Why?" Zach asked. "Because you don't like him?"

"Because he's a show-off and a clear-out and he'll probably try to cheat us and take all the glory."

"There's nothing that points to Seth being a cheater," Andy said. "Sure, he shows off. And he brags. But you have to see it from his side too. He's a new kid. He feels like he's got to prove himself."

"I still say forget it," Rachel said.

"Why? We've got nothing to lose. Give me one good reason," Andy demanded. "Just one."

Rachel threw up her hands. Then she smiled.

"You'll do it?" Andy asked.

Just then Mr. Langlin came with Andy's order.

"Here you go, Andy. One Pickleberry Soda."

Andy cringed a little. "Looks delicious, Mr. Langlin. Thanks."

They met in the stands before practice the following afternoon. Seth had his riddle sheet in one hand, his bat and glove in the other.

"How's it goin', you guys," Seth said. He put down his bat and glove. "Andy tells me we've got a deal here."

"Yeah," Andy said.

"Maybe," Rachel said.

"Let me tell you what I've got, and what I need," offered Seth. "I've got the whole riddle. Cold. It was simple."

The spaces in between Rachel's freckles started to redden. If she knew anything, she knew that Riddle Three wasn't simple.

"If it's so simple," she asked, "then why don't you explain it to us?"

"Too complicated," Seth said. "I mean—after I've got the part I need figured out, then I can explain."

Rachel turned away. "No dice," she said.

Andy frowned. "You promised you'd listen, Rachel."

"I am listening. First he says it's too simple. Then it's too complicated. Which is it?"

"It's simple," Seth said.

"Then what do you need us for?"

"You guys all grew up here," Seth began. "You know all this local stuff. Like who Oscar is. Once I find that out I've got it licked. So what d'you say? You tell me who Oscar and his friend are. I tell you how the riddle works. Do we have a deal?"

Zach held his hands in the shape of a T. "Time-out!"

Seth waited while the three friends put their heads together. Andy and Zach were for the deal. Rachel was against it. They finally persuaded her when Zach offered to take out the garbage for her two weeks in a row.

"And I'll help him to make sure it gets done," Andy said.

"Oh, all right," Rachel finally said. "On one condition. We don't let him know we're stumped."

"That's ridiculous," Zach said. "Why else would we be making a deal if we weren't stumped?"

Rachel smiled. "Just 'cause we're nice guys," she said. They walked back over to Seth, who was holding up his bat.

"I'll tell you what," Seth said. "Just to show my good faith I'll add this to the deal: You guys can use Thunderbolt whenever you like."

"What in the heck is Thunderbolt?" Rachel asked.

Now Seth looked a little flustered. "Thunderbolt is my lucky bat," he said. "My dad made it when he was a kid. It's the best bat I ever used. Honest."

Rachel was about to laugh. "You think you can get us to make a deal with some crummy old—" Andy reached behind and gently yanked on Rachel's long red braid.

"It's a deal, Seth," Andy said.

At that point, Coach Terwilliger showed up and called the kids to the field.

During batting practice the coach had them all work on keeping their heads down when they swung. Most of the Sluggers had the bad habit of looking up to see where they hit the ball before they actually hit it.

Zach was having an especially good day at the plate. Usually, he couldn't generate too much power from his skinny frame. But today he was booming them out to the outfield, one after another.

After he took his last swing he handed the bat to Rachel. "You've just got to try Thunderbolt," he said, handing the bat to her. "It really works!"

Rachel threw Seth's bat on the ground and picked up another bat. "You hit well because you were keeping your head down," she said. "It has nothing to do with that bat."

After several swings, the coach pointed out that Rachel's bat was too heavy. "Remember," he said. "It's the speed of the bat that makes the ball go. Not just the size of the bat." He suggested that she try a different bat and picked up Thunderbolt.

"Not that one," Rachel pleaded.

"It's just your size," the coach said. "Give it a try."

On the first pitch, Rachel fouled one off. Then she missed completely. From behind the backstop, Zach and Seth were watching. Rachel missed another pitch.

"This thing's jinxed!" she said.

"You're doing it on purpose!" Zach cried.

Seth cupped his hands around his mouth. "Don't fight it," he said. "Let Thunderbolt do the work *for* you."

Rachel shook her head.

"One more pitch!" the coach shouted.

Rachel decided she would swing much too easy — just to show how ridiculous all this Thunderbolt talk was. The ball jumped off her bat into center field.

"Wow!" she said. She looked back. Seth was gone.

"What'd I tell you," Zach said.

Rachel handed the bat to him. "Oh, get serious," she said. "What d'you think, this bat is magic or something?"

After practice, Rachel, Zach, and Andy met Seth in the stands. "This'll have to be quick," he said. "My mom's waiting out in the parking lot. Well?"

Andy told him as much as they knew. Oscar was

William Oscar Bloom—the man Bloom Field was named after. There was a statue of him over near the flagpole. Since he loved nature, the statue showed him doing what he enjoyed most—taking a walk in the woods with his dog. His "friends" were the animals that were shown with him. There were several of them—a deer, an owl, a gopher, a butterfly, a squirrel—

"A *skunk*!" all four of them cried when they reached the statue. It was true. The third animal down the line from William Oscar Bloom was a skunk.

"How could it be a skunk?" Zach asked. Everyone turned to Seth.

"It can't," Seth said, pulling nervously at his chin. A horn honked in the distance.

"What do you mean, it can't?" Rachel asked.

Seth stood shaking his head. "I mean—it doesn't make sense. *Skunk* is a word. But what's a *kunk*?"

The horn honked again. "I've got to go," he said.

"You can't go." Andy pleaded. "You haven't told us about the riddle yet."

Now the horn honked louder.

Seth seemed confused. "I'm telling you—it doesn't matter anymore. The r-riddle's not right."

"Of course the riddle is right," Rachel insisted. "Now tell us what it means. We had a deal, remember?"

Just then they heard a voice from the parking lot:

"Seth! Right now. We're late!"

"Listen, you guys. This didn't work out, I know. But I'll make it up to you, okay?"

"Don't bother," Rachel said. "Next time we'll know better than to make a deal with Clear Out Bradigan."

"It's not that," Seth said. "Really. I'll explain the whole thing later. I've got to go now."

And with that, he ran off, leaving Rachel, Zach, and Andy standing there next to the statue.

"So much for Oscar's skunk," Zach said.

"And our deal with Clear Out Bradigan," Rachel said. "I told you we shouldn't have done it."

Andy looked down at the ground. "Maybe you're right," he said.

7 The Little Things

After dinner that night the phone rang. "It's for you, Rachel," Mrs. Langlin said.

Rachel came to the phone. It was Andy. He was calling to apologize.

"Maybe you're right about Seth Bradigan," Andy said.

"Maybe I was wrong," Rachel responded.

"Huh?"

"Can you come over right now for a few minutes?" Rachel asked. "I want to show you something."

When Andy arrived, Rachel and Zach sat down with him at the dining room table.

"Kunk," Rachel said. "That's what did it."

"Come on, Rachel," Andy said. "Tell me about the riddle. I don't want to hear about any of your *words* right now."

"Kunk isn't my word. It's Seth's word."

Andy laughed. "Kunk isn't even a word. *Is* it?"

"Nope," Rachel said.

"That's what got Seth all confused," Zach said. "He thought he had the riddle solved. But *kunk* didn't make any sense so he thought he made a mistake."

Andy put his hands over his ears. "Would someone please explain all this to me—in English?"

Zach took out a riddle sheet. He and Rachel explained how the riddle was about knocking letters off words to get other words. He wrote the word *bath* on the sheet. Then he crossed out the *h*.

"For example, knock off the *h* in *bath* and what do you get?"

"Bat!" replied Andy.

"Something to hit at home," Rachel said. "As in, *Do this to a bath, and get something to hit at home.*"

Andy furrowed his brow. "Are you sure it's that simple?" he asked.

"What else could it be?" said Zach.

Zach wrote the word *chair*. Then he said, *"Do the opposite to chair, and get something to comb."*

"*C-h-a-i*?" Andy said. "What does that spell?"

"No," Rachel said. "Do the *opposite* to chair. That means take off the first letter, not the last."

"*H-a-i-r*. I see," said Andy. "Do it to *chair* and get something to comb. *Hair*. Hey, this is pretty good."

"Now comes the tricky part," Zach said. "Oscar's third friend is a skunk, right. But what's a *kunk*?"

"Now I remember," exclaimed Andy. "That's what Seth wanted to know. But what *is* a kunk?"

"It's nothing," said Rachel. "Because Oscar's third friend isn't only a skunk. It's also something else."

"What?" asked Andy.

"What else is a skunk?" answered Zach with a smile.

"Uh, a mammal? A rodent? Give me a hint."

"Well, what do skunks do?" hinted Rachel.

"Uh, they eat," said Andy. "They sleep. They smell."

"Bingo!" Zach said.

"Smell?" said Andy with a puzzled look on his face. "Take off the *s* and you get *mell*. So what?"

"Not smell," replied Rachel, starting to lose her patience. "Stink! A skunk is a stinker. Take off the *s* and you get the third clue. *Tinker*."

"Are you sure of this?"

"Positive," Rachel said. "Now the only question is, what's a *tinker*?"

"And for that matter," Zach asked, "what are *Chance* and *Cubs*? And what do all three clues have to do with each other?"

Coach Terwilliger asked the Sluggers to show up a half hour earlier than usual for the Rocket Raiders game on Sunday. He gathered the team together behind the dugout—and then waited for quiet.

"Who are my star players?" asked the coach when he had everybody's attention. "Raise your hands!"

Seth's hand shot straight up. Zach, Rachel, Susan Stein, and Ernie Peters also put up their hands. But they did it more slowly and much more sheepishly.

"Okay, 'stars,' step up and grab a plastic spoon," ordered Coach Terwilliger. "Then each one of you pick a teammate from the Sluggers that are left."

All the kids just stared at the coach for a moment.

They were too surprised to react. But then they got up and did just what the coach asked. Seth picked Michelle as his helper, Rachel chose Andy, and so on.

"We're going to have an old-fashioned egg race," said the coach, as he handed each star an egg. "Put 'em on your spoons."

The kids all laughed and started to make jokes. Egg races and Youth League baseball seemed like a silly combination.

"This is no joke," warned the coach. "This is a very important part of our pre-game warm-up. The race will tell me a lot about how you'll play the game."

"Then let's get to it," said Seth, suddenly quite serious. "The faster we start, the faster I win."

Coach Terwilliger explained that the so-called stars would run with the eggs on their spoons. Their teammates would run alongside them—hands cupped inches below the spoons. This way, if an egg fell off the spoon, they could catch it before it splattered on the ground.

"Ready!" called out the coach. Each star steadied the egg on the spoon.

"Get set!" he continued. Each teammate crouched down with upturned hands forming an egg safety net.

"Go!" yelled Coach Terwilliger. And they all took off for the oak tree about fifty feet away.

Ernie Peters's egg hit the ground right away. Luis had stopped to scratch his nose a second before the egg fell. Susan Stein changed course too quickly. So nobody was there to save her egg. And Zach, looking for an edge, had changed hands without telling his partner.

It came down to Seth's team and Rachel's team. They were dead even at the halfway point. Then Seth bolted out in front of Rachel—and his own teammate, Michelle. He was five feet from the oak tree when his egg went splat.

But Rachel didn't win either! When she saw Seth take off, she forgot about playing it smart. She suddenly quickened her pace and stretched her spoon arm way out toward the finish line. The egg rolled off her spoon and hit a diving Andy on the left wrist.

"Just as I suspected," said Coach Terwilliger. "Lots of stars, but no winners."

Seth and Rachel were both about to say something. But neither did.

"You're all working on the *big things*," continued the coach. "Better hitting, fielding, and pitching will make you better players. But even the best players need to do the *little things* to win."

"Like what?" asked Seth, feeling that the coach was talking directly to him.

"Like working to make the players around you look good," replied Coach Terwilliger. "Back each other up. Talk to each other on the field. Do what's good for the team—not just what's good for you."

All the players stood silently for a while. Several, including Seth, were slowly shaking their heads. They were letting the whole "little things" idea sink in.

"I can do the little things," Seth finally said, breaking the silence.

"You mean *we* can do the little things," answered the coach. "Okay? Now show me!"

* * *

The Sluggers had trouble doing anything at first. They were quickly reminded why the Rocket Raiders were the undefeated league champions. Rachel was struck out on three straight, sizzling fastballs. Marty Franklin followed by watching two more lightning pitches go by before whiffing on an off-speed pitch.

Now Seth was up. He wanted to show the coach something good right away. But two mighty swings produced two big strikes.

Coach Terwilliger called Seth over to the dugout. "Choke up on the bat," he said. "That pitcher is too fast."

"Don't worry about me," Seth said. "I never choke up. Besides, I can hit this guy."

"Maybe you can," the coach said. "But if you choke up, you'll get the bat around quicker. That'll give you a better chance of making ball contact. And that's what we need right now. We have to show this guy *we* can hit him."

"It doesn't seem like such a *big thing* to me," Seth said.

"It isn't, Seth," the coach said. "It's one of those *little things* I was talking about. The ones that make the big things work."

Seth went back to the batter's box. *What the heck*, he thought. *I'll move my hands a couple of inches up on the bat.*

The next pitch came speeding in over the plate. Seth reached out and swung.

Crack! The ball shot over the infield and into the gap between the left fielder and center fielder.

The Slugger bench exploded.

As Seth pulled up at second base, he seemed to be totally caught up in the team spirit. He was jumping up and down, while waving his fist in the air.

"Okay, Sluggers!" Seth yelled. "We can do it!"

Seth kept on cheering after Michelle's long single to right brought him home. But his new attitude didn't mean the end of the old Seth.

"How's that for teamwork!" he called to Rachel as they picked up their gloves.

"Huh?" she said.

"Remember?" yelled Seth. "The best players help their teammates look better. I just helped the whole team look better."

Rachel rolled her eyes. "I knew it!" she screamed. "I knew your team spirit wouldn't last."

The Sluggers' lead didn't last, either. In the bottom of the first, after a pop-out and a strikeout, the third Raider batter slashed a double. When the next batter hit a sharp one-hopper to first, Marty Franklin leaped to his right and made a brilliant stab at the ball.

That should have been the end of the inning. But none of the Sluggers remembered to help Marty out. Neither Zach nor Luis, the second baseman, went over to cover first base. With nobody to throw to, Marty had to run with the ball to first. The runner was safe by two steps.

It was just a little thing, but when the next batter walked it seemed bigger. And after a triple, a single, two errors, and a double, it seemed absolutely huge.

By the time the inning was over, that *little thing* turned a 2–0 Sluggers shutout into a solid 5–2 Raiders lead.

When the team came back to the bench the coach shook his head. "Now you know the secret," he said. "Little things turn into big things. Little things *are* big things in disguise."

For the next two innings, the Sluggers tried to help each other with the little things. Seth backed up Susan in center field and kept a misjudged line drive to only a single. Zach remembered to cover first when Marty ran in to get a bunt down the first base line. And Rachel was there to catch a high pop-up for Luis when he lost it in the sun.

Going into the fourth inning, the score was still a respectable Raiders 5, Sluggers 2. At this point everything became a little unreal. First, Rachel walked and Marty bunted safely. Then Seth connected with a fastball and sent it high over the left-field fence.

"Pinch me," Zach said to Andy, as they watched Seth and the other runners round the bases. "I think I'm dreaming."

"You're not dreaming," Andy said. "We just tied the score against the Rocket Raiders!"

The Sluggers celebrated. Everyone jumped out of the dugout and danced around. They acted like the game was over.

In the bottom of the inning, Robin Hayes went in to pitch and the Raiders brought them back to reality with three straight singles. Then, with bases loaded, the Sluggers panicked. They just stopped doing the little things.

The Raiders' batter dropped a bunt down toward third. Michelle ran in from third and Andy raced out from behind the plate. They met at the ball. Michelle had nobody to throw to at home. And, when she turned and fired to third, there was no Slugger at the base to make the play.

Those two little things cost the Sluggers three runs. But the Raiders weren't finished. They loaded the bases again.

The next batter then hit a long blast to center field. Susan Stein, who was running for the ball, stopped when she heard a familiar cry.

"Clear out, everybody!" Seth boomed.

"Not again," Susan cried, kicking the dirt angrily.

As Seth got to the far edge of the warning track, he brushed up against the chain link fence. Suddenly he was stuck! His pants were tangled on the fence. Yet, somehow, he still managed to catch the ball.

The catch *was* great. But now Seth couldn't get loose!

"Throw the ball!" the coach shouted.

Seth tried, but he was so tangled up he could barely move.

"Throw it in!" everyone shouted.

But only Rachel took action. As she raced over to

Seth, the Raiders' base runners suddenly realized that they could tag up on their bases and run. They also realized that Seth was trapped!

By the time Rachel pulled the ball from Seth's glove, one Raider had already scored and a second base runner was rounding third. Rachel fired to Marty, who threw a perfect strike to home. Andy tagged the surprised runner just before his foot hit the plate.

"Yer out!" the umpire barked.

"Now that's what I call teamwork!" the coach cried. "What a play!"

Unfortunately, it was not nearly enough to turn the game around. In the fourth inning, the Sluggers went three up and three down. The Raiders then scored two runs, making the score 11–6.

In the bottom of the fifth, a few more little things cost the Sluggers another two runs. And by the end of the game, the Raiders had a comfortable 13–7 victory.

But the Southside Sluggers had scored a kind of victory too. For half a game they had played even with the Raiders. They knew if they could do more of the little things they could win some games. And they could definitely beat those Mudsharks next Saturday.

On the way home Seth caught up with Andy, Rachel, and Zach.

"Okay, you guys," Seth said. "I'm gonna help you. You saved me out there today. So I'm gonna save you."

"What do you mean?" Andy said.

"On the fence," Seth said. "When I was stuck,

Rachel got the ball. Her throw and the out at home plate saved me from looking really bad."

"So?" asked Rachel, wrinkling up her nose.

"So," Seth said in a soft voice. "I'm not used to being helped like that. It makes me nervous."

"So?" Rachel said.

"So I was thinking," Seth said. "If you can do a little thing for me—like help me out when I'm stuck on a fence—then maybe I can do a big thing for you."

Rachel's eyes narrowed. "Like what?"

"The riddles," Seth said. "One more try. For the fourth riddle *only*. After that we're on our own again."

"Great!" Andy said, sticking out his hand.

But Rachel stopped him. "Not so fast," she said. "What makes you think we need you to help us with the riddles?"

"Hey," Seth said, "teammates help each other out. Remember? And besides, if we don't do it I'll feel like I owe you something. And I don't want that to happen. Do you?"

Rachel thought it over. "You win," she said. "It's a deal."

8 Where the Teeter Totters

"How about that guy," Rachel said. "First Seth Bradigan doesn't want to work with us. Then he does. Then he doesn't. Now he does."

"Give the kid a break," Andy said.

"Yeah," Zach said. "I think he might really help."

"Like the way he helped us on Riddle Number Three?" Rachel replied.

"He *did* help on Riddle Three," Zach said. "Remember? He was the one that gave us *kunk*."

"Big deal," Rachel said.

The three were waiting at their favorite tree. After the game, they had agreed to meet Seth this morning at nine o'clock. Since it was vacation time, they figured they'd get an early start. It was now twenty minutes after nine. Seth's bike was parked nearby, but he was nowhere to be found.

At 9:30, they decided to get started. If they discovered anything important, they'd tell Seth about it when he came.

"Andy," Rachel said, "why don't you do the honors?"

Andy took out his sheet and read the fourth riddle:

> *"Over land, beyond the water*
> *In a place where teeters begin to totter*
> *On one side three, on the other one*
> *This isn't fair, this isn't fun*
> *It won't be there if you look for ever*
> *So try it again, now isn't that clever?*
>
> *"After you solve riddles one to four,*
> *Here's a way for you to score:*
> *STICK TO YOUR POSITIONS."*

Then Andy smiled. "Okay, Sherlock," he said to Rachel. "You got any ideas?"

"Zach?" Rachel said.

Zach blew a bubble. "*Over land, beyond the water.* That's the playground. The *land* is the big sledding hill. The *water* is the pond. You need to cross both to get to the playground."

"Good," Rachel said. "Andy?"

"This is too easy," Andy said. "The playground has seesaws. Seesaws are teeter-totters. It must be the seesaws."

"Exactly my own thoughts," Rachel said.

"Mine too," Zach said. "Why don't we go over there and take a look?"

"What about Seth?" Andy asked.

"If he shows up, he shows up," Rachel said. "We can't wait here all morning. Come on. Let's go!"

* * *

The playground brought back fond memories to all three Sluggers. Once they had come here often to swing on the swings and play games. That, of course, was before they discovered baseball.

From a distance, Zach pointed out the seesaw arrangement. There where were three seesaws on one side of the benches, and only one on the other.

"That's it," Rachel said. "*On one side three, on the other one.* That's the riddle!"

"Good work," a voice said.

The three Sluggers turned around.

"Seth!" Andy cried. "Where've you been?"

Seth walked out from behind the tree.

"Right here," he said. "What took you guys so long?"

"What took *us* so long?" Rachel said sharply. "We were supposed to meet at the oak tree, remember?"

"Oh, right," Seth said. "I was early so I decided I'd come over and have a look around."

Rachel eyed him for a moment. "Well," she said. "What did you discover?"

"Not much," Seth said. "How about you guys?"

Seth suddenly stood motionless and put a finger to his lips. "Here they come again," he said.

"Who?" Zach asked.

"Sh-h-h!" Seth whispered. "Some kids with Mudsharks hats were snooping around here. Keep quiet."

The four of them waited silently for several seconds.

"This is ridiculous," Rachel said. "What do we care if some Mudsharks see us?"

"Haven't you heard?" Seth whispered. "Some of the Mudsharks and Raiders supposedly have all four riddles solved. They might even know where the cards are."

"So?"

"We'll watch what they do," Seth said softly. "Maybe they'll give us some ideas."

"They're leaving," Zach whispered.

"See," Rachel said, as they watched the three Mudsharks cross the bridge over the pond, "they don't even have the foggiest idea what they're doing."

"Do we?" Zach asked.

The seesaws were painted red with yellow seats. A heavy iron support post connected each seesaw to the ground.

"You think we're going to learn something from climbing on a seesaw?" Rachel asked Seth.

"We'll never know until we try," Seth said. "Andy, Zach. Why don't you two get on up there?"

"This is pointless," Rachel said.

"Maybe," Seth said.

Andy and Zach got on and started seesawing up and down. Meanwhile, Seth went around to the iron support post to investigate.

"Take a look at this, Rachel," he said. He pointed to the words "Swenson's Levers" printed on the side of the plank. "See the way the post covers up some letters when the plank goes up and down? What do you make of it?"

"To tell the truth, Seth—I think we're barking up the wrong tree here. We should be paying attention to the *arrangement* of the seesaws. The *three on one side and one on the other*. This Swenson's Levers stuff is dumb."

"Oh, yeah?" Seth said. "Well I think the three on one side and one on the other side stuff is dumb."

The two were glaring at each other when suddenly Zach pointed in the distance.

"Don't look now," he said. "Here they come again across the bridge."

"Who?" Andy asked.

"The Mudsharks," Zach said. "Isn't that Chip Hoover?"

"Relax, everyone," Andy warned as the three Mudsharks entered the playground.

The Mudsharks were still feeling pretty cocky about their recent winning streak. They were especially into reminding their rivals the Sluggers about who won the last time out.

"Well, what do we have here?" Chip said, with a mean-looking smile. "You guys giving up baseball and taking up seesaws and swings?"

"I hear you Mudsharks have all the riddles solved," Seth said, ignoring Chip's little put-down remark. "Is that true?"

Chip pulled on his lip. "Maybe," he said. "You Sluggers asking for our help?"

"Maybe what?" replied Seth, again ignoring the last part of Chip's answer.

Chip leaned over and stared Seth right in the face.

"Maybe we solved the riddles and maybe we didn't. Why should we tell you? How about you four—makin' any progress?"

Seth didn't back off a bit. "Maybe," he said. "That's our business!"

"We're doing okay," Andy added.

"There is one thing we're pretty sure of," Seth said.

"What's that?" Chip asked.

"We're gonna beat you guys on Saturday," Seth said.

"You think so?" Chip said.

"You can bank on it," Seth said, his eyes fixed right on Chip's.

"Come on, Chip," one of the other Mudsharks said. "Let's get going. Leave them to play on their seesaws."

"We'll be seeing you then," Chip said. "Make sure you show up."

"Right," Seth said. "Saturday. Don't *you* be late."

"Oh, we won't," said Chip.

"That's the way to handle them," Zach told Seth after the Mudsharks were gone.

"Hey," Seth said, holding his palms up. "What else was I gonna say?"

"I don't know," Andy said, shaking his head. "That Chip Hoover's an awful good ball player. Maybe it's not such a good idea to get him all stirred up like that. What d'you think, Rachel?"

"Let's get back to the riddle, okay?" Rachel said.

For the next hour the four of them tried everything. They got on seesaws and got off them. They looked underneath, around, and alongside them. They combed through the sand on hands and knees. They even got up in a tree for a better view of the situation.

"Nothing," Andy said glumly.

"I think this riddle is much harder than the other three," Seth said.

"What'd you expect?" Zach said. "It's just like the riddle says: *It won't be there if you look for ever.*"

Suddenly Rachel gripped Zach by the arm.

"Wait a second!" she cried. "Maybe that's it."

"What's it?" Zach said.

"It's in the wording," Rachel answered. "All this time we've been looking for *forever*. We should be looking for *ever*."

"I don't get it," Andy said.

Seth took out his riddle sheet and unfolded it.

"In the riddle, the word *forever* is spelled as two words," he said. "See: 'for . . . ever.' "

"So?" Zach said.

"It means the word *ever* has something to do with the clue," Rachel said. "And I know what. Follow me."

She dashed over to the seesaw and pointed out the words "Swenson's Levers."

"There!" she said. "Right in the middle of *Levers* is the word *ever*. It's got to mean something."

"Quick!" Seth said. "Everyone up on the seesaw."

"Not this again," Zach groaned.

"This time," Seth said, "you three get on that side together—and I'll stay on this side alone."

While Seth held his side steady, Andy, Zach, and Rachel boarded the seesaw.

"It'll never balance," Andy said. "We'll just crash to the ground and you'll shoot up in the air."

As soon as he got on, Seth's half of the seesaw shot him straight up.

"See," Andy said. "I told you it wouldn't work."

"That depends on how you look at it," Seth said. "This is what I see: three on one side, one on the other."

Andy smacked himself on the forehead.

"Of course!" he said. "The riddle! That's it!"

"Andy, can you read what it says in the center of the board?" Seth asked.

Andy leaned over and reported, "The *Swenson's* is covered up by the support post. All that's left is *Levers*. No, wait. The *L* is covered too. It says *evers*."

"Bull's-eye!" Seth said. "You see it? It won't be there if you look for just *ever*. *So try it again. Again* means more than once. What happens when you try *ever* more than once?"

"You get a bunch of *evers*?" Zach said.

"Right," Seth said. "The plural of *ever* is *evers*. And that's the clue. *Evers!* Now isn't that clever?"

"That is pretty clever," Andy said.

"The Great Bradigan strikes again!" Seth cried. Then he let out a roar of fake crowd-noise. "Can you believe how fast *I* solved this thing, once *I* got rolling?"

Rachel grumbled something under her breath.

"What was that?" Seth asked.

"So much for teamwork," she said.

9 Hot and Cold

Zach's Orang-u-tang Chip Cooler made a slurping noise as it hit bottom. "Ah, that's good," he said. "By the way, it was great that we solved all four riddles. But we still don't know what the commissioner meant at the end of the riddle sheet: 'After you solve riddles one to four, Here's a way for you to score: STICK TO YOUR POSITIONS.'"

"I don't know what it means," Rachel said, looking out the ice-cream shop window. "But we've only got one day to solve this, you know. Tomorrow's our game against the Mudsharks, and then the card hunt is over. Once more, Seth's late."

"So?" Andy said. "All Seth's doing is lending us his baseball card book. After that he goes back to working on his own. And we go back to working on our own."

"Thank goodness," Rachel said.

Andy sipped his Bubble Gum Freezer. "I think you're jealous of the way he solved Riddle Four," he said.

Rachel frowned. "*He* didn't solve Riddle Four. We *all* did. Remember? He just tried to take all the credit."

Just then Seth came bounding through the door, tossing his baseball card book on the table.

"Let's get a move on," he said. "Time to go."

"Go?" Zach said. "Where are we going?"

"We're not going anywhere," Rachel said. "Our deal's over, remember?"

"Look," Seth said. "I've got a hot lead. You guys want to help track it down, or not?"

"Where is it?" Andy asked.

"The Lotus County Museum," Seth said. "And we need to go quick. Before it closes!"

On the way over Seth explained how he'd called everywhere asking about baseball card shows. The last local show had taken place four years before. The Lotus County Museum's monthly newsletter had an article about it.

"And get this," Seth said. "The assistant remembered that Commissioner Brady's cards were in that show!"

"Wow!" Zach said. "You think they're the same ones?"

"Why not?" Seth said. "If you were in a baseball card show, wouldn't you bring your best cards?"

As they walked up the steps of the museum, Zach noticed three familiar figures rounding a corner.

"Hey, wasn't that Chip Hoover and his Mudshark pals?" he said. "I wonder what they were doing here."

"I don't know," Seth said. "But I've got a good idea. Let's get up there!"

* * *

"May I help you?" the assistant asked.

She showed the four Sluggers where the back issues of the newsletter were stored. After searching for several minutes the Sluggers came back to the desk.

"It's not there," Seth told her.

"That's impossible," the assistant said. "Only last month all the back issues were refiled—and none were found missing." But after rechecking, she confirmed that it was true. The newsletter was gone!

A few minutes later, the Sluggers were back on the sidewalk.

"Some hot lead that turned out to be," Rachel said.

"Hey," Seth said. "It's not my fault it's lost."

"How do we know it's lost?" Andy asked.

"How else could it just disappear?" Zach said.

"What about Chip Hoover?" Seth said. "Did you notice he was carrying that knapsack?"

Andy shook his head gravely.

"I can't believe Chip would take the newsletter," he said. "That would be stealing!"

"I agree with Andy," Rachel said. "Anyone could have taken that newsletter. Even Seth."

"Why would I take it?" Seth said angrily.

"I don't know," Rachel said. "Just to lead us on a wild goose chase. To get us working with you again."

"Look," Seth said. "Our deal's over. I came today to lend you guys my baseball card guide book. I figured you might find some cards that fit the clues. That's all! I thought I might help you out with some extra information about the card show. I guess I was wrong."

With that, he stormed away down the sidewalk.

"Wait!" Andy cried. "What about the guide book?"

"Keep it!" Seth shouted, without even turning around. "There's nothing in it, anyway!"

Back at their favorite oak tree, Zach paged through the baseball card guide book. "If we could only find out *who* the players on those cards are," Zach said. "Then maybe that would give us a clue as to *where* the cards are hidden."

"What we need right now is a strategy," Andy said.

"The trouble is," Rachel said. "We don't have a strategy. All we have are four words. *Chance. Cubs. Tinker.* And *Evers.*"

She wrote the words down. The page in her notebook looked like this:

Clue	Meaning
Chance	a risk? accident? fate? a person's name?
Cubs	baseball team name? baby bears? other babies?
Tinker	try to fix things? a person who makes repairs? a name?
Evers	more than ever? a name?

"Okay, what do you see?" Rachel asked.

"Words," Zach said. "Weird words."

"I see names," Andy said. "*Cubs* is the name of a team. The others could be names of players."

"Then how come we didn't find them in the baseball card book?" Zach asked. "We've gone over every player who ever played for the past fifty years."

"Maybe it's someone from more than fifty years ago," Andy said.

"Fat chance of that," Zach said. "The book doesn't go back more than fifty years."

Suddenly Rachel's eyes flashed.

"Zach," she said. "You got your library card handy?"

Zach nodded. "Why?"

"We're going to the library," Rachel said. "We need to check out a baseball book."

"But we already *have* a baseball book," Zach said.

"Just hurry up," Rachel said. "Time's wasting."

On their way to the library Rachel pointed out that if the cards were *more* than fifty years old, they wouldn't be in this particular baseball card guide.

"But they might be in one of those old-time baseball books," she said. "So let's see if we can find one."

It was a good plan. Unfortunately, the library did not have many old baseball books. After combing the stacks all they found was one book about twenty great stars from baseball's early years. There was also one other book about the history of baseball. But it had already been checked out.

As the librarian handed Zach his card back Zach asked, "This other book—about the history of baseball—do you remember who checked it out?"

"As a matter of fact, I do," the librarian said. "It was just today. A young boy. About your age. Baseball cap. Sneakers. I could look up the name for you but the computer's down. If you come back tomorrow—"

"Tomorrow's too late," Zach said. "But thanks for your help anyway."

They took turns reading the book. They learned about Babe Ruth, Ty Cobb, Josh Gibson, and Walter Johnson. They found several great old players who were Chicago Cubs. But none of them were Tinker, Evers, or Chance.

At dinnertime Andy started for home. "Well, I guess this is it," he said.

"Boy," Rachel said. "This is becoming a real double disaster. Not only do we *not* find the cards but it looks as if either Chip Hoover or Seth Bradigan will."

"We don't know that," Andy said.

"What do you mean?" Rachel said. "Chip's got the newsletter. And Seth has the book about baseball history."

"Andy's right," Zach said. "We don't know if either of those things is true. Anyway, let's go early tomorrow, okay? Maybe we'll find something."

"Yeah," Andy said. "Let's hope so."

At eight o'clock that evening, Andy rang the Langlin doorbell. "Sorry about coming over so late," he said. "But we have to call Seth. Now. That book he has is our only chance."

"We don't need him," Rachel said. "And anyway, how do we know he even checked it out of the library?"

"We have to find out," Andy said, handing Rachel the phone. "Now dial," he said firmly.

"*What book?*" Seth said over the phone, when Rachel asked about the book he'd checked out of the library.

"Come on, Seth," Rachel said. "Don't play games with me. We know you checked out a book about baseball history from the library today."

"I tried," Seth said.

"What d'you mean you tried?"

"I mean after I checked it out I went back for a minute. I put the book on the table so I could check on something. And when I came back, it was gone."

Andy, who'd been listening in, took the phone.

"Is this really true, Seth?" he asked.

"On my honor," Seth said. "I set it down, and then two minutes later it was gone. And the weird part is— except for the assistant librarian, no one else was even around!"

"We have to get that book," Rachel said, after she'd hung up the phone. "Chance, Tinker, and Evers are the names of players. I'm sure of it now."

"Then how come their names aren't in the baseball card book?" Zach asked.

"Their cards are more than fifty years old," Andy said.

"What about the book with the twenty great stars?" Zach asked. "It goes all the way back to nineteen hundred."

"That's just it," Rachel said. "Maybe Chance,

Tinker, and Evers weren't such big stars. Maybe they were just good players."

"That's what I don't get," Andy said. "Why are the cards so valuable if the players weren't even superstars?"

"Maybe they *stuck to their positions*," Zach said.

"What?" Andy asked.

"That's what it says on the riddle sheet," Zach replied. "*Stick to your positions*. Maybe Chance, Tinker, and Evers were players who were famous for sticking to their positions."

"All I know is we better stick to getting that history of baseball book," Rachel said. "Maybe it can tell us how Chance, Tinker, and Evers could be famous without being superstars."

"We won't get that book in time," sighed Andy. "Tomorrow is our game with the Mudsharks. When the game ends, the card hunt ends. It's just *too late*!"

"No, it's not," Rachel said. "Tomorrow morning you two guys check out bookstores for old-time baseball books. I'm going back to the library to read encyclopedias and biographical dictionaries. We'll meet at the field at game time."

10 Stick to Your Positions

The commissioner made two announcements before the game began. First, no one, so far, had found the cards. And second—at two o'clock, after the game, he would make a presentation to any players who did find the cards. If no cards were found, three names of Youth Leaguers would be drawn from a baseball hat filled with names. They would each get a card.

"Well?" Rachel said to Andy, when the three Sluggers met up. "Find anything in the bookstores?"

"Nothing we can use," Andy said glumly. "How 'bout you—find anything in the library?"

"Nothing!" Rachel said. "But guess who I saw there? Seth! I heard him ask about a book that deals with the history of baseball. Then the librarian gave him something. He put it in his pack. I don't think he noticed me sitting there."

"You think it was the book?" Andy asked.

"What else could it be?" Rachel said.

"Great!" Andy said. "Let's go take a look at it."

The three found Seth doing warm-up exercises.

"Hey, everyone," Seth said, before they could say a word. "I feel sort of weird about what happened with that baseball history book. Just to show what a good team player I am—I'll tell you what. If I get my hands on it between now and two o'clock—we'll share it. Okay?"

"Sure," Andy said. He looked down at Seth's backpack. There was a bulge in it about the size of a book.

When they were out of hearing distance Andy shook his head. "I can't believe he'd lie to us," he said.

"The only way to find out," Rachel said, "is to get a look inside that backpack."

At that point the coach clapped his hands together. "Okay, let's do the little things today," he said. "If we play well, we *can* beat the Mudsharks. Robin, you'll pitch the first three innings. Then, Zach, you'll be fresh to bring us down the stretch."

With no score in the top of the first, The Mudsharks had a runner on first base.

"Still think you'll beat us, Andy?" Chip Hoover said, as he strutted to the plate.

"Yup," Andy said calmly.

"Well, forget it," Chip said. "We're not the Raiders, but we're good enough to crunch the Southside Whiffers twice in a row."

"Hey, Chip," Andy replied. "Been to the Lotus County Museum lately?"

"What's that supposed to mean?" Chip said, just as the pitch came in.

"Strike!" yelled the ump.

Chip hit the next pitch to left center field—between Susan and Seth. As the two closed in, the Sluggers tensed up. Everybody was waiting for the cry of "Clear out!"

But it never came. When Susan dove for the ball and missed, Seth came in behind her. He took the ball on one hop and fired to second. Chip had to settle for a long single.

Unfortunately, the next batter hit a hard shot down the right-field line. Chip came in to score. But Robin shut them down after that. She struck out two and caught a pop-up to the mound. The Sluggers came up to bat, down 1–0.

In the dugout, Rachel launched her plan to get a look inside Seth's pack. In a voice that was way-too-loud she said, "Hey, Zach, you got any extra gum?"

"You don't even chew gum," Zach said, with a puzzled look on his face. Rachel kicked his foot.

"'Course I do," she said. "M-m-m, strawberry! Anyone else like some? Marty? Andy? How 'bout you, Seth?"

"Sure," Seth said.

"Want a few sticks for later, too?" Rachel asked. "I'll stuff a couple of pieces in your backpack."

"Okay," Seth said. "No, wait. Toss 'em over here. I'll stick 'em in my pocket."

Rachel frowned.

"Nice try," Andy whispered, as Rachel grabbed a bat before going up to the plate.

Rachel led off with a bouncing single up the middle. A groundout by Marty moved Rachel to second. Then

Seth hit a low rocket that knocked the shortstop's glove off. Seth was safe as first and Rachel came around third to score.

Michelle and Susan both flied out. But the inning still ended in a 1–1 tie. The Sluggers saw that as a good sign.

The score remained locked at one for two more innings. Robin was pitching well today, and the Sluggers were backing her up. Michelle made a fine play on a bunt. And the rest of the infield was handling all the grounders that came their way.

"Way to go out there!" the coach told them. "We're starting to play like a real team today. Now get out there, Zach, and do your stuff."

The Mudsharks had a runner on first in the fourth inning when Zach knocked down a line drive up the middle. Ernie Peters ran in from shortstop to pick up the ball and throw the runner out.

"Nice backup, Ernie!" the coach cried.

On the next play, however, Ernie slipped on a loose piece of new sod and couldn't make a throw to any base. One run scored. Then, after a flare single to right field, the Mudsharks went ahead, 3–1.

When the Sluggers came to bat, Rachel, Zach, and Andy were still trying to find out what was in Seth's backpack.

The bubble-gum trick hadn't worked. They tried asking for a wristband, but Seth didn't have one. Finally, when Zach asked for a plastic bandage strip, Seth caught on.

"What's going on here, anyway?" he asked.

The three Sluggers looked at each other. Finally Andy spoke up.

"We want to look inside your backpack," he said. "You offered to share your book about the history of baseball with us. Well, time is running out. Start sharing!"

Seth shrugged as if he had nothing to hide. He opened the pack. Out came dirty socks, a half-eaten apple, worn-out batting gloves, and finally—a book!

"*All About Frogs!*" Zach groaned. "That's not it!"

"Of course not," Seth said. "I told you I didn't have it. This is a book I picked up for my sister."

"But you were there," Rachel said. "At the library. You asked about the baseball book. I heard you."

"I was just asking if they'd found it yet," Seth said. "I figured a librarian must have taken it by accident and filed it for reshelving. So I went back to the library to have them search for it for me."

"And did they find anything?" Rachel asked.

"I don't know," Seth said. "They said if they find it, they'll call. Then my mom'll drive it over."

"Wow," Andy said. "I don't know what to say. We were really out of line."

"I'll say," Seth said, as he picked up Thunderbolt and took a practice swing. "I never lied to you guys or tricked you."

Seth took his anger out on the baseball. He slammed the second pitch way past the left-field fence. As he crossed home plate, all the Sluggers were there to greet him. Their pats and cheers made him feel a whole lot better.

"Hey, Seth," Zach said, after the game continued. "You really came through there. We're only down one run now."

"Yeah," Seth smiled. "But it looks like I'm going to strike out with the baseball card hunt. Without that book, we're all finished."

"Wait!" shouted Zach. "Isn't that your mom's car pulling up?"

"It sure is!" yelled Seth.

The Slugger at bat ended just then. Seth had to take the field before he could speak to his mother. With two innings left, the Sluggers were down 3–2. And they still had three baseball cards to find.

In the top of the fifth, the Slugger teamwork reached a new level. First Rachel backed up Susan in right center, holding a drive off the fence to a double.

"Way to go!" Coach Terwilliger cried from the bench.

Then Seth made a perfect relay from the left-field corner to Ernie. The shortstop cut the ball off and threw to third to nab the runner by a whisker. Finally, Andy and Luis combined on a pretty pick-off play at second.

"Fantastic!" the coach said, when the team came back to the dugout. "What got into you guys?"

"We're in a hurry to get back to the history of baseball," Zach said.

"What?" asked the coach.

It didn't take long to find it. Shortstop Joe *Tinker*, Johnny *Evers* at second, and Frank *Chance* at first.

They were the original Chicago *Cubs* double-play combo in the early 1900s. In a sense, they *invented* the modern double play. And because they worked together so well, they were famous as a *team*—not as individuals.

"Are you thinking what I'm thinking?" Rachel asked, after they'd read the book.

"The bases," Seth said. "The cards have something to do with the bases. First. Second. And out near shortstop."

"Wait a second," Zach said. "The clues can't be on the field, remember? It says so on the riddle sheet. And the commissioner was real clear about that."

"H-m-m," Rachel said. "Let me work on this."

While Rachel worked on the clues, Andy struck out swinging for the fences. Then Zach quickly popped one straight up to the catcher. That made it two outs with nobody on base.

Rachel then forgot about the clues long enough to lash a sharp single to center. Marty Franklin followed with a triple to bring her home. The Sluggers had tied the score at 3–3 with a two-out rally.

Now Seth was up. He looked over the outfield. He had already hit two long flies and a home run today.

"Time-out!" he called, and went to the coach. "I've got an idea," he said. "They're playing so deep, all I need to do is dump one over the infield."

"Wouldn't you rather hit one out?" the coach asked.

Seth smiled. "Well, yeah," he said. "But that might be hard. Dumping one would be easy. What d'you think?"

"I think you're catching on," the coach said.

Seth went back to the plate and took a ball. Then a strike. On the third pitch he chipped one over second base. Marty scored easily to put the Sluggers ahead, 4–3.

"Do you believe it!" Zach said, pounding Andy's back. "We can really win one here!"

"I'll tell you something even more unbelievable," Rachel said. "The game's almost over and I haven't heard anyone say the words 'Clear out' yet!"

After the third out, the Sluggers dashed onto the field. All they needed now were three outs to win the game. But they only had the same three outs left to find the cards and win the hunt. Nobody wanted to depend on a chance drawing.

The Mudsharks quickly put runners on second and third with only one out. Coach Terwilliger called time-out to meet with Zach and Andy on the mound. At this point, Seth dashed over to Rachel and whispered to her. She nodded. He pointed to first base, then second, then the shortstop area.

"Go for it!" Rachel said.

Chip Hoover was up next. "I'm gonna win this ballgame," he told Andy, as he stepped up to the plate.

Chip worked the count to three and two. Then he hit a fastball a mile high behind shortstop.

It looked like an easy play. Everyone waited for Ernie to make the catch. Suddenly he ducked away, threw up his hands, and cried, "A-a-a-a-h! The sun!"

He was blinded!

Everything stopped. The Mudshark base runners

didn't know what to do. The umpire froze. And the Slugger infielders couldn't decide whether to cover their bases or go for the ball.

There was only one person who had a chance at the ball. That was Seth, who'd been backing up the play.

"Clear *o-o-u-u-t-t!*" Seth roared.

But as he came storming in, he slipped on the new sod. On his back, he reached up to catch the ball just before it dropped in for a hit. Still on the ground, he flipped the ball to Zach.

Zach wheeled. He looked at second. There was no play there. He turned to third—no play there either.

"*Home!*" Rachel cried, from right field.

Zach whipped around and fired home to Andy, who put the tag on the speeding Mudshark.

"Yer o-u-t-t-t!" the umpire bellowed.

A double play! The Sluggers had won the game!

Now things seemed to freeze again. While most of the Sluggers rushed to congratulate each other, Seth Bradigan headed straight for Andy and Zach.

"Quick!" he said. Then he whispered something in their ears.

A moment later, Zach, Andy, and Seth pulled off another big play. Zach ran over to first base, undid a flap under the bag, and pulled out a slip of paper.

"You have just found Card One: FRANK CHANCE," the paper said.

Andy ran to second and pulled out a slip that read, "You have just found Card Two: JOHNNY EVERS."

Finally, Seth reached under the new sod behind

shortstop to find the third slip, for JOE TINKER.

* * *

A few minutes later, the commissioner took the microphone. "I'd like to read you a poem written by Franklin Adams in the year nineteen-ten," he said. "It was reprinted in the *Lotus County Museum Newsletter* four years ago:

"These are the saddest of possible words,
    Tinker to Evers to Chance.
Trio of bear cubs and fleeter than birds
    Tinker to Evers to Chance.
Ruthlessly pricking our gonfalon bubble,
    Making a Giant hit into a double.
Words that are weighty with nothing but trouble,
    Tinker to Evers to Chance.

"A great poem about a great trio of players. By the way, I removed the newsletter from the museum a few weeks ago just for this occasion."

"So no one stole it after all!" Rachel cried. "It was the commissioner!"

One by one, the commissioner called the names of Zach, Andy, and Seth to accept their cards.

Zach and Andy both said thank you. They also mentioned how Rachel had done a big part of the detective work.

"Thank you," Seth also added when it was his turn. "But I don't want to keep this card."

The commissioner looked surprised.

"You don't?" he said.

"No," Zach said. "I think it should belong to our team. We're starting a team collection. And this will be the first card in it." He turned over his baseball cap and put the card in it. Then he looked out to Andy and Zach.

"What do you think, you guys?" Seth asked.

Andy and Zach came over and put their cards in the cap. Then Rachel and the rest of the Sluggers joined them.

"Now that's what I call team spirit," the commissioner said. "I now declare the Great Lotus Pines Baseball Card Hunt over!"

Afterward, Zach and Andy were still a little puzzled.

"I've got one question," Andy said. "How come the cards were on the field? Didn't the riddle sheet say they couldn't be on the field?"

"No," Rachel said. "It said there would be no *clues* on the field. Not cards. That's what fooled everyone."

"Sure fooled me," Andy said. "How'd you figure it out, Rachel?"

"I didn't," Rachel confessed. "Clear Out did. Sorry. I mean Seth."

Seth's face reddened.

"The card hunt was a team victory," Seth said. "We really did make a good team on the field and off."

"Well put, Clear Out, old buddy," Zach said, patting Seth on the back.

Then all four Southside Sluggers laughed out loud. And they walked off together talking about their great double victory.

Coach Terwilliger's Corner

Hi there, all you Sluggers!

Collecting baseball cards can be an exciting hobby. Here are tips about putting your collection together.

How to Get Started
Buy some baseball cards! Start with just a few at a time. They're easy to find. Over the years baseball cards have come with hamburgers, hot dogs, cookies, potato chips, popcorn, breakfast cereal, cupcakes, candy, and, of course, bubble gum.

How to Recognize Valuable Cards
In general, there are three things to look for:

1. **Old cards**. For example, a common card from 1990 is worth 3 cents; a common card from 1952 is worth $20.

2. **Superstar cards.** A Darryl Strawberry or José Canseco card is worth much more than the average player's card.

3. **Rare cards.** When a card is old, a superstar, and rare, it is worth the most of all. A rare 1952 Mickey

Mantle card is valued at $6,500. An extremely rare 1909 "T206" Honus Wagner was sold for a reported $100,000.

You can find out more about the rarest cards by going to a reputable baseball card dealer or looking in *Topps*™ *Baseball Cards* guide.

How to Treat Your Cards

The condition of your cards is very important. Each card is given a collector grade. Collector grades range from Mint condition, to Excellent, Very Good, Good, Fair, and finally Poor. A card in Mint condition can be worth up to 20 times more than one in Poor condition. So keep your really good cards in protective plastic.

Above all, remember to enjoy your cards as much as you can. Read them. Play with them. Trade them. Learn about baseball from them. And have fun.

That's all for now. See you in the next Southside Sluggers Baseball Mystery. Until then, play ball!